37 Bridges and Other Stories

Aamer Hussein was born in Karachi and studied briefly in Ootacamund before moving to London at the age of fifteen in 1970. After graduating from SOAS, he studied philosophy and languages. His works of fiction include collections of short stories – notably *The Blue Direction* and *Insomnia* – and the novels *Another Gulmohar Tree* and *The Cloud Messenger.* He is also an essayist and a professor at the University of Southampton.

37 Bridges and Other Stories

Aamer Hussein

HarperCollins *Publishers* India

A version of this book was first published in Pakistan by
ILQA Publications in 2014 as *The Swan's Wife*

First published in India in 2015 by
HarperCollins *Publishers* India

Building 10, Tower A, 4th Floor, DLF Cyber City, Phase II,
Gurugram Haryana – 122002, India
www.harpercollins.co.in

2 4 6 8 10 9 7 5 3

P-ISBN: 978-93-5177-034-3
E-ISBN: 978-93-5177-035-0

2 4 6 8 10 9 7 5 3 1

This is a work of fiction and all characters and incidents described
in this book are the product of the author's imagination.
Any resemblance to actual persons, living or dead,
is entirely coincidental.

Typeset in 10.5/14.5 Goudy Old Style at
SURYA

Printed and bound at
MicroPrints India, New Delhi

Contents

The Man Who Stood Still

Dear L:

I just read your poem. 'The man who ran away'. Yes, I recognise myself as the guest to whom, after too much champagne, at a party on the deck of a boat on the moonlit Bali sea, with gilded butterfly dancers flitting around us, you told a story about a man who brought you close to death with his silences, his longing for someone who'd died.

You didn't know then how well I knew him. And at the end of the poem, when 'I' ask what you felt for the man ... no, let us save your reply for another page. I thought I would respond by writing something about you. I'm no poet, so I'll just write you this tale, and send it to you in a letter. In a language you won't understand.

So. Listen:

This happened nine years ago.

1

Remember the evening M told you: No two lovers are ever alike. I know you've had a bad experience; but don't make memory into a cage. You'd just left your husband then. And you were far away somewhere, hiding in a village by the sea, writing your poems. No one knew where you were. M, too, was drowning: but he'd lost someone to death. You were wrapped up in anger, and he in grief.

But you wrote to him often, perhaps because he was ten years older, and a storyteller. Who knows why people think storytellers are wise? We only look around us, record and reflect what we see. Or we wound ourselves to write in blood. We rarely understand a thing.

With your exchange of letters, you grew closer: when you came back from your seaside refuge, you began to see him, nearly every day. But he didn't want anything from you or ask you for anything. You were like a flash of lightning he'd seen from the corner of an eye on an empty rainy beach. And that's all he expected you to be: a flash of lightning in a rainy sky at night.

Meeting someone every day can be dangerous. Togetherness becomes a habit. It was summer, too.

Days were sultry. Evenings were long and white. (Sometimes, he sang to you: he'd been a singer once, but stage fright had frozen his throat.) Mornings came early. You said you were becoming unused to being alone. You visited a new place every day: a park. A river. The sea. And you talked: of anguish, of expectations.

Then you had to part for a week. He was going away. You weren't happy. You said: I have a premonition about this. When you come back it'll all change. We'll be caught up in our business, each of us, in the long, long business of living.

That was probably the day he told you he'd die when he was sixty. It wasn't something he willed or wanted: he was just sure he would. You said there wasn't any point in a friendship that would last only twelve years: he was forty-eight. Let's just leave it here. He laughed, and you wiped away a teardrop. You smiled. But you were pensive.

He was away five days, in an artificial city in the Arabian Gulf, on an artificial beach, and he didn't really think about you. He wanted to escape from all those thoughts of the past or the present that made him sad or weary. Your memory stayed with him like those flashes of lightning he saw one night on that artificial beach. But he remembered your hands, your pale eyes, and your curly brown hair, which he said you should always wear loose: your hair that reminded him of the woman who had died, though perhaps he never told you that.

But you were right. Everything changed when he returned. You told him you were going away the next day: you wouldn't have a moment to see him. You were visiting a sick friend far away. He was startled: he'd thought he would find you waiting for him. How selfish we are, even if we don't intend to be.

You left, went far away. And the flow of his life became stagnant. You still met but often you seemed spent and spoke little. You lost your temper with him over a trifle: a trivial observation about a book you'd praised to him and he'd abandoned.

It was then, during those days, that you began to miss your husband. At times you wept; at others you were full of rancour. And that's when M told you that not all men in love were the same, nor was every woman. You were silent, but a sense of estrangement was growing between you, something he had never sensed before. But you still met, less often perhaps, and the days went by, and the evenings turned russet.

~

So your story is meant to be about me, you said when I met you last week and translated my tale-in-a-letter for you, word by word, over little plates of meze and a magnum of arak.

I recognise the shadow of the man you call M, you said: the man who ran away from love. And I recognise some moments in his life. I remember his song about a woman who counted the crimson flowers she had planted in a patterned ceramic pot and fed the seven sparrows that lived in the eaves of her house while she waited for her dead lover to come home from the war. I remember how his voice made my flesh crawl with its hoarse loveliness. But this story of yours is just a fairy tale. A conventional romance. Sunsets and russet evenings and there's probably an autumn moon somewhere. You even named the lovers after a classic pair; I recognise the initials. Archetypes. This could be about anyone. So where am I in this?

Remember, I replied, when we met at one of those free literary jamborees, on the flamboyant isle of Bali, you heard me talk about his work on a platform, how I admired him, not in spite of, but because of, his difficult reputation.

Ah, and as I said at the start of my story, I was going to remind you of something. At the end of the poem, when 'I' ask what you felt for the man, you say: I might have loved him once.

So. Keep listening. There's a twist. I know you don't like the mention of russet evenings, but one such evening is a part of your story.

2

On such a russet evening, a world-famous philosopher came to speak at M's college about the psychological effects of war at a time when wars had changed the shape of the world you came from. A time when moving around the city was difficult for Muslim boys, or those who looked vaguely Arab: they were stopped in various parts of the city, and one innocent who was not even Muslim had been shot in an incident.

After the talk, a young man came up to greet M. He was of medium height, slim and curly-haired, with yellow eyes. He asked if you'd both join him and his colleagues for a drink. M looked at you for a response and before you answered he dismissed the boy with a terse phrase: Another time. He took your arm and walked away.

And as you sipped beer at a nearby bar after the talk, you asked him: Who's the pretty little boy, seems to be a fan of yours. Don't think he's read more than a little of what I have written, M said. Some years before, the young man – let us call him Z – had sought him out, saying: Would you write my story? It is very interesting. He came from the north of his country (which I won't name in my story); he'd moved to the capital to study. His father was dead; his mother and his brother had saved up enough to send him abroad to study law, but he wasn't receiving enough money from home to live on. He rented a little room in the house of a Muslim family but he'd had to borrow money from friends to pay his landlord. He started driving a taxi to pay his debts, and stopped attending classes regularly.

M wasn't able to help him financially in any way, nor did the young man have a story M wanted to tell. His was the plain tale of all those millions who leave their lands in search of something better; when they arrive at their destination, they find nothing. But Z would call M from time to time or come to visit him. And one day M asked him, so what's so special about you that I should write your story?

He said, I could do anything to live here, I could even lie, I could say I've committed a sin, a crime for which my savage tribe will execute me if I go back to my country.

But that's preposterous, M responded. If your family ever belonged to a savage tribe, they certainly forgot their links with it a long while ago. For one thing, you've almost abandoned your studies; for another, you spend your valuable mornings sleeping and your nights driving around because you're acquisitive and fond of expensive things, gadgets, mobile phones and tight jeans. Finish your studies first: get your degree, it's a matter of months now. Then you can talk about leaving or staying on and buy whatever you want to.

As he spoke, he heard the false ring of his didactic and avuncular tone; he was beset by mixed feelings of compassion and disappointment for the young, plain, simply dressed boy who could almost be his son. He had played witness to the boy's yearning to give up his home and the willingness to turn away from his family because of his dread of stepping backwards.

Some days later, M had a call from someone who said he was a friend of Z's. Z hadn't been attending classes, he had been working illegal hours, fourteen hours a day, was in trouble with the authorities, he'd be sent back if he didn't get himself together. Could M vouch for his character?

M wasn't going to refuse, but what could he have said? Yes, lots of people worked illegal hours, and he thought that the rules for casual labour should be changed, the ratio of supply and demand was unequal and there were so many kinds of hunger to satisfy, but he couldn't really say that in his position.

Yes, he told the caller, if needed I'll tell them that I know he's an intelligent young man and a hard worker, but financial problems have stopped him from studying as he should ... and if in future I can be of help, let me know.

Later, M heard that Z had been very ill, had a mental breakdown; he couldn't have been sent away in that condition. But while he was recovering, it seems he had found a very good lawyer who'd persuaded the authorities that if he went home he'd be conscripted, or that was the version that was current. He'd been allowed to stay on and had gone back to his studies with some financial aid to complete them. There were other, competing stories about lies, about deceptions, about a rich protector, but those weren't M's business. And one day when M met him in the corridor, Z said: You always wanted to write my story, you can now ...

So tell me, M said to you, what can I say about him? That the lies he told caused him to have nightmares, to dream about his brother's body lying decapitated in the debris of a bombed building, about his mother running in the empty lanes of a devastated city? And to run from his own fears, of the open city streets, of stark daylight, of men in uniforms, of trees that looked like gallows in the night?

You fell silent.

~

You fell silent. Or did you quarrel then, as you had started to do? Did you talk about refugees and the harsh lives they faced in those inhuman times, or about the lies and subterfuges of illegal migrants, or the phrase 'savage tribes', which you believed the boy would never have used? Or was it the ghost of something else, of the boy's story of dispossession, perhaps of deprivation, that walked between you? I don't know.

I didn't start anything, no, you said. I remember the boy, yes, and the way he fawned on the man you call M, and how M shook him away abruptly. No, it wasn't me. It was him. Seeing the boy saddened him. Telling the refugee's story made him worse. He was silent, surly, all the rest of the evening.

I haven't written much more, I told you. I lost my way here, and whatever else I wrote seemed to fall into clichés, or to belong to another story. But I can tell you what I think happened, later.

3

You left the bar and began to walk, slightly out of step, the silence between the two of you as sour as bad red wine. Then he began to talk, in a rushed but halting monologue, about the woman who had died young and left him, he said, quoting a poet, to sleep in the sleeve of grief because he hadn't known what to make of her gifts when she was alive. He said that he'd lived in the expectation that someone's love would heal him, calm him, and when she'd died, his own guilt left him bereft. It was six months now since they'd taken her body home.

You looked up at the sky and pointed at the moon which was the colour of mottled blood, you looked up and said: Look! The black moon! And you spoke of how, in your language, that mottled moon was considered unlucky for lovers, even cursed.

He told you then that he wanted you, needed you, stayed awake at nights talking to you, he talked to you in his sleep, wondered if he could spend the rest of his life without you.

You told him it was too late to talk of these things; that if you ever could have cared - and yes, there'd been a chance, way back, at the start, in summer - he'd been too withdrawn, too sunken in the sleeves of his own grief, he'd never even touched you except to graze your cheek with his cold lips when he said goodbye. And now there was someone else, a young man with sparse blond curls and blue eyes that were slightly crossed, and a tiger body you desired, though as yet you'd done nothing, nothing, but it was only a matter of days before ...

Say no more, he said.

You walked on together in silence.

~

I remember the night, you said, that night in November, the pompous philosopher and the mottled moon. But I was leaving for Helsinki the next morning and said I didn't want to be late at the airport. It was midnight and it wasn't a night to talk about love. I would have heard him out another day. He turned and walked away in the dark. He left me alone on a lonely street. When I looked back, he was running.

Not true. He kissed you at the entrance of the station before he ran. And he often runs when it's cold.

You lit a cigarette.

Is that what he told you then, you hissed.

Of course you've never known, then or now, how close I remain to the thought of him, that even in his absence I can see his heavy soul in his eyes when they're suddenly naked. The man who stands still and never runs. Who never touches anyone until they touch him.

And he kissed you.

I don't remember the kiss, you said.

He kissed you. Then he ran. From the cold bitter taste of your lips.

You put down your glass and stood up to leave.

So that's it then, your story.

Stay, I said to your departing back. You've yet to hear the end.

4

When he'd said goodbye to you at the station, he began to walk; he was a long way from home, but he couldn't bear the thought of public transport. The November night had fallen, and it was cool. He found himself in step with a group of young people in evening dress, obviously on their way back from a celebration. A silver-haired young woman from among them in a red dress and an open fur jacket broke away from them and asked him for a cigarette. Join us, she said. We're going to another party. He smiled, shook his head, and walked away.

Two blocks down, he reached for his cigarettes and found an empty space where his wallet had been. Had the young woman put her hand in his pocket, taken it as she spoke to him? Or had he dropped it on the street?

He retraced his steps. Nothing. Even if he had dropped it, someone would have picked it up within the space of a moment or two. Library cards. Identity cards. Bank cards. What else was in it? He had to get home to cancel what he could immediately.

He had his keys, some change, and his travel card in his pocket. Best to take a bus, he thought. As he reached the high street he ran to where a bus was pulling out. It would take him near enough to where he lived. He jumped on; the conductor swore at him under his breath.

He went to the upper deck. It was empty of the usual throng of sad-eyed night workers who travelled home at that hour. Only one man, his face covered with a shabby black cotton jacket, lay on a seat at the back.

In spite of the autumn weather, he was sweating; his jacket clung to him, feeling like a bearskin. He shrugged it off and laid it beside him. His shirt was soaked.

He shut his eyes for what seemed like a moment. When he opened them again, he saw a man with a very red face leaning over him.

It's the last stop, the man said. Wake up. You have to leave the bus here.

He rose, then bent to look for his jacket. Gone. Next to him was the reeking ragged jacket of the man he'd seen earlier, and an empty beer bottle. Now he had no keys, no cigarettes, and no travel card either. He got off to find himself in a place he didn't recognise, a suburban street of darkened doors. One shop at a corner still had its lights on: a twenty-four hour grocery. He thought of buying cigarettes but remembered he had no money. When he had orientated himself by turning around, he realised that he was near the entrance of a park quite far away from his neighbourhood; but if he walked through it, he'd be on the road that led him halfway home.

The park was dense with evergreens; in their nocturnal forms he felt that there were animals and birds hiding, snakes, wolves, turkeys, bulls, as if they had escaped from the nearby zoo. In a moment, they would emerge from the shadows. He was shivering in his silk shirt without a jacket, though the night air wasn't very cold for November. His feet were hurting. The full red moon loomed overhead and in its light he remembered reading that in the park they'd built a glass house in which there was a miniature simulacrum of a beach, artificial sand, sea represented by a salt-water pool complete with artificial waves, reflected in a mirror that made it look infinite; people began to swim there in November and visited it throughout the winter months. Was he imagining this, or had he also read that on certain nights of the week it stayed open for twenty-four hours, and entrance was free? Was tonight such a night?

He turned down a path that said 'To the pools'

and found himself in a strange, abandoned space that looked like the backyard of a factory. He found that his eyes could discern certain forms in the dim light of a distant building. He saw that he was in a children's playground, with swings and slides and toy horses. He was exhausted now and knew that to ready himself for the walk home he would have to rest a while. The dark red moon came out again from behind a very dark cloud. He sat down on a bench, took off his shoes, and, just to pass the time, he began to sing. The only song he could recall was a plangent ballad you used to hum to him, in a language he half-knew. One by one, as he hummed, the words and the cadences of the ballad came back to him. He sang, louder and louder, his higher notes echoing in the stillness. He was unafraid of being heard in this abandoned space. He sang about the bitter river of blood that flowed from a wound within him, and that other wound, more bitter still, of your last kiss on his lips.

He closed his eyes when he'd repeated the chorus three times and opened them, after what seemed like a long blink, to see a milky first light bathing the trees in the courtyard of his block of flats, where he was sitting on a low stone ledge beneath a plane tree. His shoes were beside him, and his jacket was slung over his shoulder. Magpies hopped from branch to branch, pigeons rested on stone ledges, and sparrows searched for crumbs in the courtyard littered with the detritus of the night.

He checked his pockets: keys, travel card, wallet. Cigarettes, yes. He took one out of the packet and lit it. His cold bed could wait. Sitting barefoot on the ledge beneath the tree, he began to sing, softly: a song about a boy who jumped off the roof of an empty train and walked for miles down a broken bridge to the wide white desert where he sat beneath a giant cactus and pierced his forefinger on a thorn to write a letter on the breast of a friendly robin who swore to sing his birthday message to the careless girl he left behind.

Two Old Friends on a Stormy Afternoon

'Look at the rain,' Dr Kazi says. 'No electricity for hours on end. The traffic's crazy. Getting here in this torrent was an ordeal. More of this and we won't be able to meet for lunch tomorrow.'

He taps the ash off his cigarette onto the tiled floor, though there's an ashtray beside him.

'No girls in bikinis today,' Colonel Jami says, peering out at the empty pool. 'No sun for them to bathe in. Can you believe it? My niece was here in a bikini last week. She said she was too pale and was suntanning! In my youth, we'd have called her dark and told her to stay out of the sun.'

'I know. I was there. They say the storm's coming here.'

Through a curtain of rain, the garden's still visible; beyond it, white-capped waves. A young woman, blonde and tall, sweeps by, twinkling her fingers at them. Her shoulders are bare, her legs revealed almost to the knee in short white trousers.

'That's old Burhan's wife,' Jami says. 'Looks younger every day and she's been married at least ten years. I saw her in a swimming costume last week. Look at her clothes. And yesterday she wrote a letter to the *London Times* defending Islamic headgear–'

'Did you hear what I said? They think the storm's going to reach us soon.'

'God's punishment, they say.'

'Where do you think I live? I've been watching TV all morning, and hearing what the bigots said. Received ideas. That's what you're repeating. Punishment for what? I'd have thought someone like you–'

'Let me tell you about Burhan and his wife. You know he has a son who's almost her age? Well, one day he came home from a trip abroad and found his son's clothes in her bedroom. He got a gun and shot the boy in the leg–'

'That's not what I heard,' Kazi says. 'The boy's a good ten years younger. She brought him up like a son. Spoilt him. The boy had a fight with his best friend over a girl. The father rushed him off to the Gulf before he got into any trouble. You've been watching too many soap operas. Anyway, let's go back to the table. I want some of those lamb chops. Last time we were here there weren't any chops when we went back to the table.'

'Biryani for me,' the colonel says. 'You should learn to appreciate local cuisine instead of hankering after foreign–'

'And what about you?' The doctor nudges his companion. 'Let's admit it, the very world you and I live in is foreign. Cars. Fans. Mobile phones. Cash machines. Girls in bikinis, though I don't know how long that will last, given our current rate of progress towards perdition. Or paradise, should I say. And when did you stop drinking your double whiskies? After your pilgrimage to that shrine near Multan? Karim' – he beckons to a white-clad waiter – 'keep an eye on our table?'

They go to the buffet to fill their plates, then return to sit at their table, in the covered veranda overlooking the garden. Beyond the low wall, the sea is grey and turbulent. A single boat bobs on the water's surface; it seems suspended in mid-move, its red sail dimmed by the rain. On an overhead screen, three men with embroidered caps are asking for donations for victims of the storm near the coast.

Starve, starve, feed the wretched, redeem your sins. A food pack will take you halfway to heaven. A tent will take you all the way.

~

'I can tell you where that money's going,' Kazi says. 'Into someone's pocket, and it won't be the victims who–'

'Don't be cynical. We live in such a beautiful country.'

'With the most awful people.'

'You know what your problem is? You see the dark side of the moon. Our young only talk about feudals and fundos and terrorists. Look at the progress our people have made. Doctors. Scientists. Sportsmen. Women moving ahead in every field–'

'Well, let me tell you I know people who've built houses on the Mediterranean with money they stole from donations and aid. Next you'll be saying that democracy brings chaos and we should never have voted the general out,' the doctor says. 'And just four years ago you were berating him for allowing corruption and creating misrule.'

'You know I left the army in '75, when I came back from that Indian camp in Bareilly and I'd lost nearly four years of my life. I wasn't even fifty. But you have to admit there's something to be said about our army. Ayub's heyday, once he'd settled into power; now that's what I call a good time. We had values! A golden age I call it ...'

~

They've finished their food, and, as usual, they beckon to the waiter to ask him about the day's dessert.

A burly man in cream-coloured shalwar and kameez comes up to greet them, raising the tips of his fingers to his forehead.

'Did you hear about Asad's son?' the colonel asks.

'No.'

'Well, you know Asad had been having an affair with Pasha, that singer in the shampoo ad. His wife was going crazy. She said she'd leave him if he didn't stop seeing her. Then their son came back from Harvard. Somehow, the next thing you know is that Pasha's out of the father's life and seeing the son. And you know what? Pasha isn't even a girl.'

'You mean she hides her age?'

'Not her age,' the colonel says. 'Pasha's not a woman, she's a man in disguise. Can't you tell? No breasts, no hips–'

'But that's an old story. Someone borrowed it from a novel. A French novel. It's been told before. The truth is that Pasha made a blue movie and–' the doctor says.

'A blue movie? You watched a blue movie?'

'Come on, old man, I'm joking, and you're right, Pasha does look like a boy. And you, my friend: you should write soap operas. You seem to know all the plots. Just think, with the stories I could tell you–'

'I did publish a book of poems once.'

'A pamphlet privately printed for your fiftieth anniversary.'

'No! Not that – that was only an invitation card. A book of poems. In Urdu. I was twenty and in my final year of pre-med. Full of hope and courage! But that's all so long ago.'

'You joined the army. I was still at boarding school in Dehradun,' Kazi says.

Karim, the waiter, comes to clear away their plates. 'Tea or coffee, sir?'

He knows, but he always asks. Coffee for the colonel, green tea for the doctor. Once, long ago – how long ago? – Karim worked in the clinic Kazi still owns, though he hasn't practised for some years now.

'But you didn't really know me then,' Jami says. 'You were – what, sixteen? Speaking of stories, you keep saying you're going to tell me about your last summer in Wimbledon.'

'Surely I've told you about London already. And that was – what, five years ago?'

They light up, Jami his cigar, Kazi a filter-tip. The sound of the wind seems, for a moment, to have relented slightly.

'Five years ago? So tell me again. I've forgotten.'

'Not much to tell. Ali and Mandana were busy all day as usual and I spent a lot of time going for walks. Then I twisted my ankle and had to stay home a lot. The neighbour would drop in when Ali and Mandana were at work and she'd tell me how she'd once been a famous singer. Her name was Valentine Voss. She was probably ninety. She lived all alone in an attic flat that she'd furnished like a little jewel box. I'd visit her for cups of tea sometimes. And she'd say: Look at this country, there are thieves and fare dodgers and scroungers on the dole. It's a wonder you all still keep coming here for slim pickings! It must be so nice where you live, sun and sea and sand ... so when are you going home? And your son? We've got too many foreign doctors here! Don't they need young doctors in your country? Don't you want them to come home and take care of you?

'Then those boys from a northern town bombed half of the London Underground and the city was in chaos. And that night I had a dream. I dreamt I'd been in jail for a long, long time for a crime I hadn't committed. When I came out and went home, my wife was covered in a white veil from head to foot. And so was everyone else. Men and women.'

'Veiled men?'

'No. Men and women all in white. I thought someone had died. All hail the Revolution, they chanted, and I didn't know what revolution they were talking about. Thank God you're free, they said. Thank God we're all free. Then I woke up, and in my dream I wished I was dreaming that I wouldn't see the people in white again ...'

'More tea, coffee, sir?' The waiter's hovering.

'You're off the point now,' says the colonel. 'Get on with your story!'

'Well, a day or two after the bombings, I went down to the pharmacy for some Calpol and who do I see but Mrs Voss, struggling with two heavy shopping bags? Hello, she said, I left my shopping trolley at home. I took the bags from her hand. Visitors to our country, she said. Foreigners abusing our hospitality! We should have sent them back thirty years ago when that nice man called Powell said they'd take us all over if we let any more of them in. And look at us now! Men with bushy black beards. Women in veils, their faces covered like bandits. Keeping their shops open all night and selling stale food. Living off our charity. Telling us what to do. I think she'd forgotten where I was from.

'And then I said, you have people like my Iranian daughter-in-law, and my son, both working as doctors for your National Health Service when they could make so much more at home, with a private practice like mine. Both over fifty, and working something like twenty-four hours a day! I keep telling them to come back. She must have known then she'd upset me. But, doctor, you're one of us, she said. They need someone like you to teach them all to be like you. I kept silent. But then I started thinking. I thought about the boys who'd so wantonly killed others and then killed themselves. What were they doing? Were they really jihadis? Who believed in heavenly beauties and rivers of milk? I don't think so, not for a moment. Weren't they reacting in frustration to want and need? Mandana worked in the north and she said the young men there lived on the margins. I'd always thought suicide bombing was a cowardly act. And then I thought how brave they must be to blow themselves up, but such misplaced bravery, such a waste, and yet they paralysed the world. To what avail? What did they do for you or me? I have to wait months for a visa to see my son, and I couldn't, at my age, be bothered to go back. As for my son, he said that if he wanted to go to almost anywhere in the world he had to wait for weeks.'

'Doesn't he have nationality yet?'

'He'd only applied that year. He's British now, says it's a relief as far as airports are concerned, but they still pick him out of the crowd to search him, if there's no one else - luckily for him, they prefer them younger these days.'

'Sir, they say the roads are closing down because of the flood.' Karim is hovering, again. 'You'd better wait for the storm to be over.'

'How dark it is already. What if it doesn't stop raining tonight? It stayed light almost all night one June when I visited Denmark. Is England like that too? But sometimes everything seems dark to me. Do you remember the woman they shot last week? Dr Masooma Usmani? And what had she done wrong? She was in a van carrying boxes of clothes to an orphanage, her office said. Was it because she belonged to the wrong party? Or the wrong religious sect? Someone said she was carrying explosives. Or guns. Or because they thought they could rob her van? Search me. She's in a coma and may never recover.'

'So you admit there's dark here.'

'It's dark everywhere. Sometimes I think of a story I heard long ago. A king was so sickened by defeat that one day he said he heard the owls call his name and say he was an unjust ruler. He took to his bed; he turned his face to the wall and his back to his subjects and wouldn't rise. His son took over the affairs of state, but there was anarchy on the street and rebellions on all the frontiers of the country. Suddenly darkness overtook the land, and night and day looked the same. The holy men said that unless the king took his place on the throne the sun would never rise again. His son went again to rouse the king, but the ruler opened his eyes and he cried out loud: I can't see. I'm blind. They summoned doctors and charlatans and holy men of all faiths to his bedside and all of them said the king's eyes were healthy, there was no reason he shouldn't be able to see with them; it was his senses that had gone blind; and while he refused to see, the land and the people would remain in darkness. Are you asleep?'

Jami checks his watch.

'Oh, time for prayers! I missed the last two today.'

Outside, the waves are lashing out and the wind and the rain wail like the soundtrack of a Gothic movie. Jami rises to go to the prayer room.

~

In his chair, eyes closed, Kazi wishes the rain would stop. He wishes Ali and Mandana were here, or at least Ali.

Jami, the man who'd had no time for things of the spirit, says his prayers every day now. Once he drank, blasphemed, and though he said he'd discovered faith in the prison camp, Kazi remembers, he continued for years to scoff at rituals. He became steadily more pious after his wife lost her sight when she was seventy. Maybe his faith has seen him through years of solitude, rheumatism and gout, emptiness.

Kazi himself has always taken a gambler's chance on eternity; if he were capable of praying he would, but all he's ever been good at is his work, and he wants to go back to work now. During his years at the operating table, removing tumours and growths and counting the days people might keep on living, or telling them their cancer was terminal, he often wondered whether somewhere, something might exist. Now, in his retirement, he still wonders. And if there is a power, has He forgotten about His creation?

Perhaps, in his dotage, Jami's right to leave it to heaven, he thinks with a twinge of what might be envy. The last notes of the muezzin's call fade and fall away. I'm going to call Ali when I get home, he thinks. I'm going to tell him to fly over. If the storm gets worse. He'll take me to the coast to help. Anyway, it's definitely time for him to come back for a while.

Singapore Jay

1

My first day at Arundales. Masud Sheikh, elegant as ever with silver hair slicked back and leather patches at tweedy elbows, is waiting at the doors when my taxi pulls up. I'm wearing uniform: light blue shirt and dark blue blazer, navy pants with pleats and blunt-toed shoes. I feel like a freak, a leftover from some other decade.

Morning, sir. (I know I have to call him that, or Mr Masud; no familiarities allowed here.)

You're sloppy, Murad, Mr M tells me, your shirt collar should be in or out and instead it's half in and half out. Didn't your father teach you to dress?

It's May. I turned thirteen a month ago; I've been

in the hilltop town a week. I came here with my father, from Bombay by air-conditioned train to Madras, then a plane to Coimbatore and a car from there, driving up the winding hill roads through a forest reserve. Looked at monkeys pick lice from each other's fur, sneezed at the medicinal odour of eucalyptus.

Even at home in Karachi, when I was seven or eight, my father would sit me on the arm of his chair and show me pictures of his dream houses in faraway places, Hertfordshire, Hampshire, the Nilgiris. We're city people, but he's always longed for green places, waterfalls, lakes, great gardens. And now, eight years later, he's made his dream come true: rented a villa beside a lake for a year in this Blue Mountain town.

It's cool even in May, but there are things happening: flower shows, dog shows, boat races, horse races. I don't even have time to adjust. The matter of school arose early. I've been missing classes for six months, so it's urgent that I start again. My father wants to send me to Lovedale, halfway down the mountain, where most of the students are the sons and daughters of white planters and expats who live in big towns hundreds of miles away.

But my mother sends a telegram from Bombay to tell us I'm to start right away at Arundales, the

Theosophist school where Mr Masud is vice principal. I'm to be a boarder, she says.

I refuse, because I hate the idea; I've never been to an all-male school before, and the thought of sleeping in a dorm with smelly boys is enough to make me rebel.

My father intervenes. I'll be driven to classes each morning, he promises, and picked up each evening.

So, here I am, on the porch of my new school. Ready for my first day. Carrying my blue-and-black striped tie in my pocket, because I never wear one.

I'm led to a wooden hall, where boys sit in rows on wooden benches, listening to recorded music. It's Carnatic music, which I enjoy, though I've only recently heard it for the first time. When Subbulakshmi's voice begins its throaty undulations – '*oooo, rangaaa shaaayeee*' – the boys nudge each other and titter, an obviously familiar ritual.

The boy who'd been sitting next to me leads me to our classroom. His name's Akash; he's pink-cheeked, pleasant, Punjabi.

You speak Hindi?

I pause before I answer.

Hmmm.

I still think of the language I know as Urdu. I left Karachi only five months ago.

At lunch, Akash takes me to the refectory, where we're fed sticky brown rice that smells odd, a thin lentil broth speckled with mixed vegetables, steel bowls of sour curd. The southern boys are eating with their fingers. I've never tasted food like this. Akash can see my surprise.

Good for your soul. He nudges me, winks.

In the afternoon, we're in the lab, dissecting frogs, mixing chemicals in vials. I've never been in a lab before. I hate it. But there are art classes, and English and history which I'm good at; Hindi too, which I've learnt, in my few months in the north, to read and write quite well, though I have no Sanskrit vocabulary.

During the break, Akash tells me he likes Biggles and Billy Bunter, neither of whom I've ever heard of; I only read grown-up novels. He offers to lend me one of his books.

2

I'm back at school in August. I'm used to the town by now; to its toy buildings with their red and green imitation Gothic roofs, its English church and graveyard, its tribal Todas.

During the holiday I made friends with the art

teacher, and spent many summer afternoons at her house, trying, unsuccessfully, to paint. I discovered the library in the centre of town, with its newish English novels on the ground floor, and its antique volumes upstairs. Enough to keep me busy, even when it rains – and when it rains in the mountains, it's a performance: shrieking winds, falling branches, grey-black days. At home, we light log fires.

Akash no longer shares my desk, or my tuck on tutorial trips to the Botanical Gardens. All through the summer I'd thought I had a friend, but then another boy told me that Akash had said he only looked after me in those first few days at someone's behest. Since everyone calls Akash 'Teacher's Pet', I can guess who told him to keep an eye on me. Our parting's mutual: maybe he withdraws because his duty's done, or maybe I do, because I'm insulted and unsure.

I'm afraid to make friends. I'm bookish, bad at making overtures. I've been allowed to give up physics and chemistry, but have to do maths and take physical geography, at which I'm just as bad. The boys I talk to are the two Rameshes. One's a Malayali science genius and inveterate Biggles and Bunter reader from Singapore. The other, a Gujarati Jain from Calicut, is jovial and obese. Singapore Ramesh tolerates Fat

Ramesh because he sees him as an incarnation of Bunter. I don't inhabit Bunterland; I probably attract them only because I'm an outsider too, and awkward. Many of the boys here come from Africa, Asia, the Gulf, and my being from Karachi just seems to be a variation on a common theme. They're too young to care about a three-year-old war, and really I'm just like any other northern Muslim boy, except for my slightly foreign looks, and what they call my fancy English accent.

The two Rameshes mean little to me when I'm away from them. But I like my maths teacher, Miss Rajalakshmi. She's young, pretty; my second-best friend at school. My best friend's my history teacher; most of the teachers here are girls, but Mrs Ratna Pratap is a plump older woman from Bhopal, who tells me my essays about Mughal emperors and empresses are as enchanting as fairy tales. I should write more, she says, and publishes something of mine in the school magazine. But when I'm home in the evenings, I never write unless I have to. I read novels and biographies and nineteenth-century plays I bring home from the library, and the *Illustrated Weekly* which Aunt Annie, my mother's writer friend, sends from Bombay. On weekends I go to every new movie at the only English cinema in town. On dry days I lie in the sunny grass on my stomach, listening to songs – Hindi film songs – on the radio, Nancy Sinatra and Lee Hazlewood on my portable, battery-operated Italian record player – singing along with them.

3

November. Often the car breaks down halfway, or the driver doesn't show up. I have to walk three miles to school, through rain, slush, sludge.

The last day of term, there's frost. Glinting on grass, luminous on tarmac. There's a party that night. The girl teachers sing syrupy tunes: '*Somewhere my love*', '*Those were the days*'. The lead singer's Saramma, the biology teacher. (She's very pretty, played tennis in a hipster sari with palla tucked in at waist throughout the term, and we all stared at her flat beige belly and her neat navel until Mrs Pratap told her to cover up.)

The lights go off. There's a hush, then a roll of drums and the wail of an electric guitar. A few notes of the piano, and a rough, high male voice singing the first lines of '*Lucy in the sky with diamonds*'. The group's behind a white screen; we see their projected shadows. The lead singer's in profile: hawk nose, curly hair. It's Jayasurya, known to all as Singapore Jay, Ramesh's maternal uncle. I've never really noticed him before. I don't like the song, even less the nasal, throaty way they sing it.

(*1968 is dying, dying.*)

We're on our way to Bombay. I'll be in a big city again, I'll see the sea, the Arabian Sea that brings ships all the way from Karachi. I'll see my mother after six months. She's coming back with us to the Blue Mountains in January.

4

We've been rehearsing a play since the new year began, and I'm in it. I've been given a double role, prince and beggar: the beggar's really the Diamond Prince in disguise. I am not the hero, Jay is. Elviro, the ship's captain, goes off to find a precious pearl for his gypsy love (played by Saramma). Diamond, in pauper's disguise, steals it from him. Jay wears boots and breeches; I am in a gold Grecian tunic.

I've grown; at fourteen I'm 5 feet 10, as tall as a man, nearly as tall as Jay. I'm popular too, with my record collection, the daring books I read, the polo necks and bell bottoms my mother's brought for me from a cousin's boutique in Karachi. The best boys in class keep my company; the Rameshes, from an admiring distance, enjoy my new-found confidence, as if they'd groomed me for success. I walk around with Sirish the cricketer and Jitendra the tennis player, the class heroes, though I have no particular friend.

But since rehearsals began, Jay and three other boys have been thrown out of school for breaking rules. They jumped over the walls at night and went into town: saw films, ate chicken biryani. Dark rumours have it that they'd been seen with the town's local slut, the Chinese restaurant owner's wife, smoking and drinking beer, eating beef and pork.

I've been offered Jay's role, and his songs. His voice is big and mine's quite small, but I can carry a tune.

Now, after the Easter break, before I have time to fit into his breeches and boots – he's taller than me, but my build is bigger, and my feet – Jay's back. I'm scared. Since Rajam, on whom I had a crush last term, left to get married, I've been friendly with Saramma; she got me to admit I'd seen the boys in town, at the Regal cinema and at the Three Kings Dosa Palace. She told Mrs Pratap. They were reported, followed and expelled. But something's made Mr M change his mind; he's summoned Jay back. Under curfew, I gather.

So he's the hero again. And I'm the villain.

5

My second cousin Adeila's come to stay. She's in trouble because she's been seeing the wrong kind of boy in her home town, Secunderabad. Her mother thinks a month in the Nilgiris will distract her. Adeila looks and dresses like a Vogue model: white op art earrings and huge white-framed glasses, mascaraed lashes, geometric Vidal Sassoon haircut, white bell-bottomed pants. Almost as smart as a Karachi girl.

She's forward too. She knows I look at her. Though I'm two years younger, she's flattered. She's let me hold her hand and taught me to French kiss, but for the last few days she's been aloof.

I don't know how to deal with her.

I've been without female company for more than a year. My mouth dries when Adeila's around, my groin tightens; when I lie in bed I smell her scent, not the Chant d'Arome she uses but something headier, hair and skin and female otherness. In my dreams I press my heart against her breasts, taste the insides of her lips. I wake up, with silvery slime on my belly or between my thighs. I sluice myself clean with a whole bucket of cold water I have to fill for myself from an outside tap; there's no running water and the mornings are cold, even in summer.

6

Adeila's on my mind the day there's a fire alarm and we have to leave the music room. Beyond the tennis court, by the well, I find myself looking straight into Jay's eyes. I flinch.

How's it going, man.

Oh, you know. And how about you.

You were really good today. When you asked me to forgive you ...

Oh, I had something else on my mind ...

Like?

Girls. A girl.

I find myself telling him about Adeila. Let's go up to the playing field, he says.

(Later I realize he noticed others staring at us.)

7

This is it. A one-off, an accident. He won't bother to speak to me again. And I'll be off the hook, won't have to tell him anything about the part I played in his expulsion.

I'm staying late at school today, for rehearsals. After classes, I go to the library to kill the tense half-hour before we start. His hand on my shoulder. He's behind me; I feel his breath on my ear.

We're running late. Come on.

What do we talk about?

Singapore, Karachi, our plans for tomorrow, the sea.

8

They're talking about you, Saramma says. Together all the time. Whispering. This sudden friendship. And he's a senior.

I'm a pre-senior. We're in the play together.

You know about him. What if he finds out you had him expelled?

I didn't. You did. He forgives me anyway.

9

We've been at the boat club, Adeila and I. It's Saturday. A fine sky, and the lake's lime green before sunset, with boaters still out on the water, trailing their fingers in its ripples. We've walked to the cinema, to see Vanessa Redgrave in *Camelot*. We stop to buy cokes and chips before we take our seats.

Come and sit with us.

(It's Singapore Ramesh. Of course, it's their evening at the movies – I should have remembered.)

It's okay. We've got a box.

No, come on.

We follow, sit down.

Five minutes later, I see Jay in shadow, overlong legs, familiar stoop, curly hair. He drops into the seat near mine.

Hi.

I feel his shoulder touch mine, the length of his arm, his knee.

(He isn't handsome, Adeila tells me later. He's dark and his lips are thick. She isn't pretty, Jay says. Flat-chested; looks like Barbra Streisand.)

10

Monday evening. I come home from rehearsal to find my parents waiting for me.

We've heard you've been mixing with the wrong sort of boy. You were with him at the cinema. (Mother.)

Who?

Don't be rude. You know who. (Father.)

He's my friend. And I'm in the play with him. Can't avoid him.

Well, your teachers don't like it. They say it's furtive. (Mother.)

And it distracts the other boys. (Father.)

Masud Bhai doesn't like it. (Mother.)

11

I know nothing about boys 'like that', as they call them. Once, I saw the two Mohans, known to be friends, fight over a ball in the playground, getting rougher and rougher until one, the taller one, just seemed to give up; the littler one straddled him, groin on groin, and ground into him, then knocked his forehead against the other boy's.

Don't mind them, they're pals, Fat Ramesh had said.

Do pals fight that way?

Come on man, don't be stupid, I mean pals like ... that.

I felt as if I'd seen something I shouldn't have.

And now:

What do we do? Do they think we're ...

Well, we hardly skulk in corners as they say, everyone sees us, so what are we hiding?

Let's show them we don't care.

12

You're letting your mother down. Making her very unhappy. If you don't leave Jay alone, he'll be sent away again. So just cut it out.

Mr M grabs my arm, nearly twisting it.

13

In the dressing room we've been given to share, I don't talk to him. He doesn't get my silent message. He keeps on talking. On stage I give the greatest performance, particularly when Diamond betrays Elviro.

Mr M tells me I showed too much hairy, muscular thigh. Mrs Pratap's summoned to drop the hem of my tunic in time for the next performance.

The second night, Jay doesn't talk while we dress. When Diamond asks for forgiveness and Elviro's meant to take my hand, he forgets his lines.

Silence takes centre stage for a moment.

(I wish I'd die. Suicide's a sin. I can't jump into the lake or hang myself; I'd be too afraid, so I pray God will just take me away in my sleep.)

14

Before the end of term I tell the Rameshes what happened.

The rainy summer passes. Adeila's gone home to Secunderabad. I've driven my parents to desperation with my lost appetite and my surly moods, and Mr M can't bear to look at me. My father sets off for England; he'd said when we came he'd stay just one year. He's promised to send for me, if only I'll wait till the next term's over. Even my mother agrees. She'd never wanted to move away from Karachi and she hates this town, the rain and the wind and the cold mountain loneliness. So I'll soon be leaving this strange place, this foreign land, for a faraway country I've never seen, a country still more foreign and more strange.

I come back to school.

Singapore Ramesh tells me:

My uncle understands. He'll wait.

Then I know what I must do.

I write to Jay. He writes back.

For weeks we exchange letters, conceal them in books left in appointed corners. We learn to break rules that were made to be broken.

Sometimes I have to wait for his replies, two days,

three, a week. I write to him and tear up the messages, swear I'll never write again. And then, as if he knows what I'm thinking, he writes another message. Sometimes his letters are long, at other they're just notes, a line or two. He signs himself 'Your loving friend'.

15

Sometimes we meet, in secret, in the lab or in the playing field on the hill. Furtive meetings, as if guilt's what we were destined for. I'm afraid to be with him now. I feel as if we're on stage again, rehearsing without a script to read from. When we part, I remember things I didn't say; it's easier, much easier, to write.

I'm defiant when we talk, but I see him chastened. He has to finish school this year; he's been loyal to me, but I know at what cost. Me, I've ceased to care: I upset everyone. Saramma hasn't talked to me since I confronted her with what I found out from Mrs Pratap – she was the one who spread stories, complained to Mr M. Most of my casual friends dropped me when I was declared dangerous company.

Singapore Ramesh keeps faith, and Mrs Pratap.

You've got to get away from here, bachche, she

tells me. This place is too small for you. It'll smash all your dreams.

16

Even when Saramma finds one of our notes in the library I'm not afraid. I'll leave here in a week or two, and Jay a few weeks after me. It's not worth anyone's while, this time, to make a scene about us. Mr Masud tells me I can take the last few days off, I needn't bother to come back before I travel north on my way to England. Still, when we leave, he's at the station to say goodbye. He'll be glad to rid himself of me, the wayward, dreamy, stubborn boy I am. It's November, purple-grey and wet again.

Jay writes just once. We're in Secunderabad. My mother finds the letter and tears it up. Anyway, I can't reply: he sent no return address. Our story's over, except when I trace it between the lines of books I read.

17

There's little left to tell. I reach London in May, a year after that first exchange with Jay. Mr Masud comes to visit, a month or two after I reach England.

We live on Bayswater Road, facing Hyde Park. I'm fifteen now, and six feet tall; already at high school, making new friends, buying cheap tickets to see films and plays with a girl from Venezuela, necking in the park. I see Mr M a few times; I call him Mamunsaheb again. He'd known me as a rebel. When I left Arundales he must have marked me off as his only failure, made excuses for my ways and my defection. But he never once alludes to my stay in the Nilgiris. It was a slip in time, an aberration, best forgotten. I am, at the story's conclusion, one of the forgiven: a member of the family, his younger sister's only son.

Love and the Seasons

1

At the age of twenty-four Umair liked listening to music, walking in woods and parks, visiting art galleries and singing. Fabi, his best friend, didn't really like walking around parks or visiting museums because on weekends when they weren't at university he liked sleeping past noon, usually with someone.

When they'd first become friends a year ago, Umair was spending a lot of time with a woman who loved feeding swans and even on the coldest winter days they'd go together to Regent's Park with bags of breadcrumbs. Sometimes Umair and the swan feeder went out dancing with Fabi and one of his girlfriends. But the swan feeder didn't like Fabi's girlfriends. She didn't care much for Fabi either.

Umair got on very well with Fabi's girlfriends, blonde Lily the designer and black-haired Sol, the Spanish student of Eng Lit. With Sol they'd even go to parks and galleries together in a threesome.

Umair and Fabi had met at their first year at university; one was studying French and the other Engineering. One evening they'd walked home together from a concert: Umair lived in Maida Vale, Fabi in Marylebone. They ran into each other in the cafeteria a fortnight later. Friendship at first sight, Fabi recollected, but Umair said that it had actually been the second.

Umair met Pia at a party Fabi took him to in the first week of the year. She came up to him and gave him a card for a vernissage in Sackville Street that was happening a few days later. The third time they met, they went out together with Fabi, drank a lot of champagne at a wine bar in Marylebone, and went back to Fabi's for a drink. Fabi offered them a room in his flat where they spent the night together. After that, Umair would usually meet Pia for dinner and go back with her to the flat she shared with her friend Barbara and Barbara's lover. He'd stay with her for a few hours, then catch a bus home in the dark. She preferred not to have him sleep over when Barbara was in town. He preferred not to sleep over when he had classes the next day.

On weekends, Pia was often away. Fabi would ring Umair on Saturdays to persuade him to go out dancing. Fabi liked to dance and drink till late and was good at picking up women. Umair didn't really like clubs but went along for a drink and a dance. He wasn't good at drinking, and wasn't in love with Pia, but he thought that a relationship with one woman was more satisfying than one-night stands. But by the time he knew how many other men Pia was seeing, he was already bored with what they had and looked forward to her being away. One day, she called, he was busy writing an essay, said he'd call back, and never did. He'd realised at some point that Fabi had engineered their meeting because Umair was on the rebound from the woman who fed swans.

Sol had lasted longer than most of Fabi's girlfriends. Strange, because they looked unsuited, Fabi very blonde and fit and Sol small and dark and skinny, while sunny Lily could have been Fabi's twin. But it was Sol Fabi felt closest to, she brought out the poet in him. Often when they were together, Sol and Umair would talk about art and films and travel. Only once, Fabi flew at them both for calling his favourite Italian diva, Mina, cheap. Later, Sol said their long debates make Fabi feel excluded.

One night at dinner, Lily remarked that, like

many old friends, Fabi and Umair behaved like a married couple. Fabi often cooked dinner for his friends as well as Umair's. Since the woman who loved swans defected, they had spent even more time together. And like many couples, Fabi and Umair spent most of their shared times with others. They didn't talk much when they were together alone, which was usually on Sunday afternoons. When Fabi noticed that sitting around and smoking and playing records was making Umair restless, they went to the Serpentine before meeting their girlfriends, together or apart.

At times, Fabi would disappear into his university life for weeks, leaving Umair with broken appointments and unpaid tickets. But Umair was making new discoveries every day. He opened a page of a Simone de Beauvoir novel and came upon a whole page that read '*j'en ai marre j'en ai marre j'en ai marre marre marre ...*', which he thought was one of the most expressive long sentences he'd ever read. He went to the library to find everything he could by de Beauvoir and Sartre and Camus. He wondered whether he was an existentialist, though he'd hardly had *marre*. He listened to Brassens and Ferre and Brel, and learnt enough songs for a concert. Rudolph, his classmate who played classical guitar, worked out accompaniments that suited Umair's slow, soft voice. They spent several afternoons planning a recital of modern chanson interspersed with pieces of classical music.

Umair had other friends. Mira the Mauritian who loved listening to him singing '*Les Feuilles Mortes*' in French and taught him new songs. Mira and Umair went to concerts together – Leonard Cohen, Joan Baez, Georges Brassens or Judy Collins. While Mira was lost in the music, Umair was dreaming of being there on stage and singing. But Umair was planning to teach languages once he'd graduated, perhaps in Italy. Mira was writing her PhD dissertation and would be teaching too when she went home. On his twenty-fifth birthday, Mira danced a Javanese dance, and because she was going away forever later that spring, he knew that was her farewell. He might have allowed himself to care for Mira if she hadn't been planning to marry her childhood sweetheart as soon as she went home, but he knew the tenderness she showed him was partly because she was missing her lover and enjoyed Umair's lavish but unobtrusive male attentions. Then there was Marjana from Kabul and her husband Tudor, who came to the examination hall to meet him with a bottle of champagne when all his final papers were done.

That summer after his graduation, Umair loved everyone and felt it was hard to say whom he loved best. That made him feel guilty, as if his affections weren't very deep. He didn't terribly miss people when he didn't see them, but he easily could pick up where he'd left off with Marjana or Fabi. He also found that in the hours between studies and friends he quite enjoyed being alone with a pile of records or a book.

He'd always been a contented fellow, but contentment, perhaps, was connected to mediocrity. What he felt that summer was closer to happiness. Happiness could only be measured against other emotions. Though he'd dealt with the defection of the swan feeder by running away to Barcelona for Christmas, filling the hole in his days with other things, he'd been sad then. When Mira and he met for the last time, he cried a little. His happiness drew something from those partings too.

In July, Umair gave his first performance of French songs at a little theatre above a French cafe on Brompton Road. He sang Brel and others and also some old songs he or Rudolph had found in old books of chansons. In between songs, Rudolph played solos. Mira had already left for Mauritius, but Fabi came with Lily and Sol, and Marjana came with

Tudor. When he saw them in the audience he remembered what Mira had said: singing was what he did best. Singing was a paradox, because the sadder the song was the more it made him ecstatic. Singing frightened him and left him drained, but when his voice dipped and soared, with the guitar's chords underlining each true note, every fear was worth it.

Tudor remarked at dinner that night in the little Polish restaurant they went to that he was in the company of exiles. Marjana's family had escaped from Kabul when the Soviets took over and before that her ancestors had come from some Tatar land. She'd grown up at schools in Switzerland and France. If she hadn't married an Englishman, she might be an exile like her widowed mother and her young brother and sister. Fabi had defected from Hungary. He was applying for leave to stay once his studies were over, but was at present stateless. His English uncle by marriage who'd helped him stay on and given him a home couldn't do anything more to keep him because he worked in Canada. Rudolph was an Armenian from Tehran.

Umair said he couldn't lay claim to statelessness. He'd come to England because he was born British. His arrival in England in his teens was theoretically a repatriation.

2

By winter, Fabi's statelessness made Umair's own London roots seem set in stone. Though Fabi got a good upper second, he was nearly twenty-six and no one was prepared to sponsor him for a job. The foreign office had no interest in his case. Sol had gone back to Santander because, she told Umair, she didn't think anything was going to happen between her and Fabi that hadn't already happened.

Fabi spent hours at home in his pyjamas, smoking one roll-up after another, listening to the Italian diva Mina.

Umair, back from a month's holiday in Delhi and Lahore, tried to understand Fabi's fears. He went over to his house with fish and chips and bottles of decent wine. He invented stories about clumsy romantic encounters, tried to make Fabi laugh, at times fearing his cheerful tone made him sound dismissive. Once he nearly told Fabi about the time he'd been seduced by Lily after a Pimm's too many at a charity fair. But there wasn't really any point because Fabi wouldn't have minded even if Lily had seduced Umair there in front of him.

Sometimes he felt Fabi was avoiding him. Sometimes he avoided Fabi when he couldn't find the words to comfort him. Then one night Fabi got slightly drunk and asked him what he'd been telling Lily, who thought Umair found Fabi's hopelessness hard to take because he didn't know what to do to help him. It wasn't true, Umair said, but they both knew it wasn't a lie either. Umair guessed Fabi knew all about his escapade with Lily.

Then Fabi hardly called any more.

3

Umair had given up French and Italian literature because he couldn't get a steady job, and enrolled as a psychology student in October, a year after he graduated. He didn't really have the courage to be a singer and felt that teaching languages was a cul de sac. In two years he would be able to practise as a counsellor. Marjana and Mira had always said he was a terrific listener: why not make money from that talent and help people too? He could sing on the side. He attended classes two days a week, and still taught English in a college in north London two other days. On Wednesdays he spent the day among the library's psychology shelves.

IRA bombs would go off in London from time to time and garbage cans were disappearing from the city's pavements. He made friends in college, but they mostly talked about post-Freudian theory. He spent more time reading Lacan in the library than with friends, old or new.

Marjana phoned about once a month to ask Umair to the cinema. She showed great interest in his psychology courses. Her marriage seemed to be coming apart. Tudor had told Umair how, when they'd gone to the south of France on holiday soon after that Polish dinner in South Kensington, she'd got a bit too close to the friend they'd been staying with. Though Tudor understood, she'd never been the same since. Marjana claimed that Tudor encouraged the affair, which she couldn't understand. Now she didn't want to look him in the eye. They'd been married since they were both eighteen. If he wasn't jealous, he could at least have put on an act.

Sometimes things still seemed the way they'd been. Marjana told Umair he ought to give a big party at home for his twenty-seventh birthday. Later they all went for a walk along the bank of the canal. Fabi came along, alone. Sol, he told Umair, was getting married. Fabi had been his old personable self for a while now, and to Umair's amazement he was canvassing for the local Tories.

Marjana had invited some friends, and among

them was a striking woman called Humaira who was doing her doctorate in philosophy from Oxford. Umair found her intriguing and knew he'd like to see her again. As they walked by the water on that yellow April afternoon, she fell into step with him and told him she needed his help to read a new feminist biography of Hannah Arendt in French.

Love at first sight, Marjana joked later. Umair and Humaira were born in the same Karachi neighbourhood a year apart, their birthdays were close and even their names. Maybe it wasn't a joke, because as summer went by, Umair waited to be summoned to Oxford, or anticipated Humaira's rare visits to London. He was in love and he brought up the subject of their relationship with her, clumsily suggesting that one day perhaps they could be married. They were sitting by the fire in her Oxford apartment in November, after he'd spent the afternoon helping her to translate passages from the biography of Arendt. She said she recognised they'd had some fine exchanges but she wasn't ready to risk anything yet because she was recovering from a long relationship with someone who had hurt her badly.

The love of others is a claw, she said, or else a trap. You find yourself in its grip and limp away when it's too late to escape.

She doesn't want to see me till spring, he told Fabi, who surfaced one wet afternoon. Fabi suggested he hadn't stated his case again with enough passion. Umair had always been too finicky in his approach to love.

Fabi hugged Umair with one arm when they said goodbye. He said he might have some news soon, he'd call in about a week.

A fortnight later there was still no news from him. No answer when Umair called.

By early December, his number responded: *No longer in use.*

At Christmas, Umair had a postcard from him, postmarked Montreal.

> *Sorry I left without seeing you or even phoning. I left in a rush. You know how it is. I'm with my uncle here now. I think I'll be staying on, good chance of a job. I'll send you a number when I know where I'm going to be.*
>
> *Love from F.*

Umair missed Fabi sometimes, but he'd already started missing him long before he left.

4

In January, Rudolph called to ask if Umair would be ready in a fortnight to be guest singer at a concert in the little theatre above the French cafe. Umair had been learning new Brel songs, and though he didn't like to perform in winter when he suffered from asthma, he agreed. He hadn't spoken to Humaira in quite a while and didn't dare to call, but he posted her a leaflet for the performance with scribbled season's greetings. On the morning of the concert, Humaira rang to say she wouldn't make it as it was misty and she didn't want to travel back to Oxford late in bad weather. But why didn't they meet next week? Lunch in St Christopher's place?

When the concert began, Umair felt his vocal cords were rusty. He'd started with a number too quiet for his voice. His choice misfired. By the third song, '*Pauvre Rutebeuf*', when he was emoting rather than singing, and audience response was slack, he wished he'd never agreed and vowed never ever again to perform for an audience. Then he saw Marjana and Tudor walk in, holding hands. He hadn't seen them since autumn because he felt embarrassed to face Marjana after he'd declared his love to Humaira who, he was sure, must have reported it all to Marjana.

He signalled Rudolph and started to sing the first lines of '*On n'oublie rien de rien*', unprepared and unaccompanied. After the first few bars, Rudolph joined him with a slightly unconventional chord, which made him change the timing of the song and sing each line with an energy that both elated and drained him. There was warm applause. When he finished his set he sang three encores, ending with a dramatic '*Ne me quitte pas*'.

5

At dinner later, he said that seeing them had reminded him of that other concert twenty-eight months ago. He'd sung the song because he remembered how he'd been with them at the same Polish restaurant and they'd all been so close.

Yes, you forget nothing, he thought as he walked away from Rudolph's car towards his front door. Things change, people leave, and you reinvent the past to remember moments of happiness that weren't always so bright, and pretend to forget what made you happy, so that you can live without the discomfort of memory. He wondered whether the memory of Marjana's distracted affair last summer had made her and Tudor bridge their gaps, and how much they'd chosen to forget.

I fell in love with you the moment we met, he'd wanted to tell Humaira that day by the winter fire in Oxford, but even love at first sight was retrospective, a reinvention. If every spark became a fire, we'd be burning all the time.

Ahmar and Anbara

1

A young man who wore a circlet of gold with a ruby that shone on his forehead saved a kingdom from an evil ogre. As a reward he claimed the hand of Anbara, the king's beautiful youngest daughter.

'Who are you?' The king asked.

'I am Prince Ahmar,' the youth replied. 'My father is the king of a far-off country, but I have sworn to stay away from my land for seven years because my brother accused me of a crime I didn't commit, and I'm not at liberty to say where I come from.'

The marriage took place with music and song and several days of celebration.

2

Now Anbara's stepmother and stepsister, who envied her fortune and her fine husband, sowed the seeds of doubt in her heart.

'Where does this young man come from?'

'To what clan does he belong?'

They wanted the ruby that shone on his forehead.

3

They sent a mendicant, who was a courtier in disguise, to tell Anbara that she must travel on a pilgrimage to a distant shrine to pray for Ahmar's health and fortune. While she was away, the stepsister attempted to seduce the prince with songs and wiles, but when her ruse didn't succeed, the women sent him a cup of milk poisoned with poppy juice. Then the stepsister crept into Ahmar's room and stole the circlet with the ruby from his forehead. Ahmar uttered a great cry, and with blood pouring from his nose and his mouth he fell to the marble floor, dead. But as he fell, the circlet she had stolen turned into dust in the stepsister's hand, and in place of the ruby, a drop of blood shone on her palm. Then she heard a fluttering of wings and looked up to see a pair of birds fly up into the air and out into the darkness through the open window.

4

Anbara's stepmother and stepsister had Ahmar's body secretly removed and buried in a wild place a day and night's journey away from the palace. When Anbara returned, the women told her the vanished prince was a trickster; an impostor who had stolen her jewels and fled to his land.

But Anbara didn't believe the women. She dressed in a suit of Ahmar's clothes, concealed a sharpened dagger in her breast, and went out in search of her missing husband.

5

She travelled for a day and a night. She encountered many obstacles, placed in her way by the other two women. As night fell, she came upon a garden enclosed in marble walls. It was a place of abundant green grass and perfumed flowers of many colours. A tall cypress tree grew there between two pools of clear blue water. She drank from one pool and washed her hands in the other. Then she sat down beneath the cypress, her head beneath its trunk, to rest a while before she resumed her journey. A round, gold, harvest moon travelled low in the sky. She was drifting into sleep when she heard two birds singing in the branches above her head. She realised she could understand their words.

'Tell me a story,' said one of the birds.

'Of what shall I sing, my love,' her mate replied. 'Of my own travels or of the world's woes?'

'Sing to me of what you saw in the world today.'

'I will tell you of the prince of a faraway country and of his bride who has been betrayed,' her mate said.

So Anbara heard them tell of her stepsister's perfidy, and learnt that her husband's life and soul lay in the ruby that was stolen from his forehead.

Then one bird, weeping, said to the other: 'Can the young man never be brought back to life?'

And her mate replied: 'The prince lies within these marble walls. His garments are this green grass and his eyes these pools of blue water. His body is this cypress tree and his hair its green leaves.

'But if his bride were to capture us, and hold us close to each other, heart to heart, and with one stroke of her husband's dagger separate our heads from our necks so that one of us shouldn't die before the other, and hold our heads above the ground where the prince lies, our blood will spill on the earth and its drops will turn into rubies brighter than the one the wicked woman stole from his forehead. Then Ahmar's heart will beat again and he'll come back to the world of the living. But if one of us should die before the other, the prince will lie asleep for ever.'

Anbara called up to the pair of birds. They flew down to her in a flash of white feathers and bent their white necks before her. Soon, she thought, she would see Ahmar awaken beside her, in the shade of the cypress tree.

Anbara took out the golden knife she had hidden in her bosom. The green grass soon grew red with the blood of the birds.

Nine Postcards and Nine Notes

(with Alev Adil)

1st Postcard from Umair

Before breakfast, I walked back to last night's perfumed bush. It wasn't fragrant now; I must have smelt a night flower. We breakfasted beneath an orange tree. By the Alcázar gate, a chamber orchestra played the Habanera from Carmen. Only oranges and songs to take away.

We are leaving Sevilla. The bus station is crowded, proletarian. My companion wants water, a ham roll, the ladies' loo. I fear we won't board on time.

A skirmish for seats, but they're numbered. We leave on schedule: midday on an August Tuesday.

1st Extract from Refika's Notebook

All those rainy London nights in Noura, Ozer, Melati and Taro, when we'd plan our visit to Granada over leisurely dinners, how we might find the heart of who we were, this long-lost European Moslem civilisation, a place fragranced with orange blossom, whose existence challenged the clichés about two unbridgeable civilisations. Should we see the palace in the early morning or should we see it in moonlight, when there was less of a crowd? We already hated the other people we'd have to share the Alhambra with. It was our imaginary palace, far from our complicated lives with the clutter of difficult divorces, custody battles, demanding jobs, family feuds and disputes about inheritances.

All that talk came to nothing. The website that sold the tickets crashed. The hotel directed us to a travel agent down a long, hot thoroughfare that stretched listlessly in the dusty heat, revealing the city's plain, everyday face, a motorway, a dusty curb, rubbish. The travel agent was not only shut, it had closed down, deserted like all the other shrouded shops.

We had Seville and the Alcázar instead. I was confused, which parts of the palace were Islamic, which Catholic aftermath? It didn't seem to matter. I couldn't imagine anyone actually living there. The gardens were loveliest. Reversed perspectives and geometries.

A weeping Madonna on the street. *Ines Rosales tortas de aceite* wrapped in greaseproof paper decorated with florid navy ink, flaking crumbs of anise and orange, tastes of North Africa on my lips. At breakfast I read *Tales of the Dervishes* by Idries Shah, its thirty-year-old cover once vibrant orange, now a faded yellow. Umair writes a postcard. 'Whom are you writing to?' I ask him.

'That's difficult to say,' he tells me.

2nd Postcard from Umair

On board, a confusing text on my companion's mobile. We try to calm each other: aren't we expected in Sanlúcar? Is there some misunderstanding? Dun landscapes fill the window.

The journey's shorter than expected. God, the vagaries of making electronic contact. My irritation makes my travelling companion laugh out loud.

I stole the term 'companion' from Pavese. In real life, friends are all that matter, but 'friend' in a narration sounds coy.

Perhaps we laugh together.

2nd Extract from Refika's Notebook

I have passed through beautiful train stations like palaces, eaten oysters in Grand Central, seen the faded Ottoman majesty and stained-glass windows of Sirkeci in Istanbul and watched gulls reeling outside the tiled splendour of Porto station, but bus stations have been tired ugly places in my experience. I've never encountered a charming one. Seville's is typical in its random concrete squalor and the pervasive smell of drains.

I spend a lot of time in bus stations in my nightmares. Bucharest, Ankara, Istanbul, Vienna, too often in the rain. Also at intersections on motorways, walking where there are no pedestrians, knowing I am once again in looks-like-Birmingham-but-is-really-Belgrade. I have never been to either city in my waking hours. My dreaming self is thirteen years old, if we suppose I sleep a third of my life. Her restless teenage soul prowls ugly peripheries and arteries, motorways and underpasses, refusing to return me to the real palace gardens I have seen.

3rd Postcard from Umair

My Spanish sister – I call her that, she calls me hermanito – is waiting at the little station. We have come to her for her birthday. She drives us to her new house: full of light as homes should be, with airy windows.

A year ago, she painted me, in oils. I'm dressed in blue and larger than life, sitting by a window of her London flat. Behind me there's a red brick wall. She complained of London's changing autumn light. Here she paints in her eyrie, in a tower. Her studio overlooks tall palms, jasmine bushes, bright flowers.

Later, with green figs, white peaches, local cheese, we drink summer wine. My sister calls it Poor Man's Sangria.

3rd Extract from Refika's Notebook

We drove down the long avenue of cypresses hidden behind the tall, dark green gates. For three consecutive Augusts we went to Sanlúcar to celebrate the princess's birthday. Umair was her guest of honour, she called him her little brother. We drove down the long avenue to the new house in the old botanical gardens.

The first year we ate in the gardens at white damask-covered tables that shone silver under the full moon. The trees were ripe with butterfly lanterns.

The second year the women danced the Sevillana, their hands a forest of swooping circular gestures, a language I almost spoke, but not at all fluently, as I discovered when they insisted on drawing me into the dance.

The third year it rained incessantly and the party was held in the old, eighteenth-century tower. Black umbrellas hung from the porch like malevolent bats. That was the year Death came with me; thought I could use the company.

4th Postcard from Umair

Satiated, seated by the blue pool now, hot as heaven. Anxieties disperse, join red petals scattered around on stone and grass. Birds dip their beak in the pool's water. In the sun's blaze, the leaves on their branches shine white. Now I think of the garden I once called home.

Shirtless, I lie on short grass. Its texture tickles my back. My companion, swimming, leaves me to my lonely thinking. (Once we shared summer ruminations. At times our silences run parallel. At others we're like strangers who don't meet.)

The cuckoo calls three times, as brazen as a rooster. Perhaps the sun estranges thoughts, reminds me of advancing age, grey hair, dull flesh. Still, in dreams, I fly before I fall.

4th Extract from Refika's Notebook

Umair is reading Pavese. The row of palms behind the tennis court is almost still. There is no breeze, yet the pool wriggles with light. I dive into the blue and try to remember something about Pavese. Razed fields, miles and miles of burnt landscape, but I can't tell if these are related to something Pavese wrote, a memory of something else altogether or my nightmares.

'He came to me young, of his own accord,' Death tells me.

I pull myself out of the water quickly, as though I could escape my new companion easily, shaking him off with the tiny droplets of water as I walk across the lawn. Soon it will be lunch. There will be gazpacho. The gazpacho is delicious. The cook is famous for it.

5th Postcard from Umair

My sister, dressed in green, is dancing the Sevillana as we enter. Two friends are with her; one dances too, the other sounds the beat with flattened palms. They are sisters.

Sunlight dapples my sister's cheekbones, flickers on her fine-drawn features. She dances with her face. I'd love to paint her like this, in her green flamenco dress, dancing. If I could paint. But she could paint herself. *Tres Morenas de Jaen, Axa, Fatma, y Maryen ...*

'What does duende really mean,' someone asked my sister at a London supper.

'Duende means talent,' she responded. 'It's not a word we use much any more.'

Tomorrow is her birthday. Her grandchildren are on holiday on another continent.

My sister, my companion remarks, looks twenty when she dances.

5th Extract from Refika's Notebook

Death is not good with dates. Time is a problem for him. All of it is happening at once. He tries not to remember everything, but it is impossible for him to forget. So busy all the time, for all of time. His to-do list gets longer and longer. There are seven billion of us now.

'I meet so few old souls these days,' he muses. 'And most of the tigers are mine already.' The wildness of beauty is on the other side now.

6th Postcard from Umair

Later, on the beach. Pavese called the sea a field. Tonight it is, a silver field.

The sky reddens, darkens, scatters stars.

'We're at the mouth of the Guadalquivir,' my neighbour says. 'The Arabs called it something like wad-el-kabir.'

'Andalusian hospitality too is Arab,' someone says.

But this is not the sea. The yellow strand is not a beach. I'll stick to my terms. Sea or river, the line of water remains a silver field.

6th Extract from Refika's Notebook

The night air is warm as blood. Dark can be both wave and particle, gentle negation. Death lights my cigarette for me, whispers in my ear. He is in his element. I am barely aware of the dinner table conversation, hypnotised by the dance of reflections on the wine glasses, huge delicate balloons teetering on delicate stalks. Another covert Sevillana, the hands gesturing, lighting cigarettes, the raising and lowering of the glasses. I hear myself telling the table about the barrel signed by Faiz I had seen in the winery today. My voice sounds very far away to me. The princess tells the story of Faiz's visit to Sanlúcar.

7th Postcard from Umair

We eat water creatures: anchovies and anemones, cockles, langoustines and bream.

My neighbour speaks to me of ragged love and separation. My mind and tongue unlock their Spanish. We are, at fifty, childless. My companion, eleven years younger, has a son.

'You should have a child, the two of you,' my neighbour says.

'Ah,' I tell her, 'but we're not lovers.'

'We're best friends,' my companion adds.

'Do you still feel Pakistani,' the Venezuelan to my left asks me.

'I do, when I feel anything at all.'

The Venezuelan drones on.

'Muslims in Europe are a demographic problem. In Andalucía, I hear, they want to reclaim ancient sacred places. They should be loyal to their country of adoption. Wouldn't you say?'

'I guess I'm a Muslim in Europe too,' I say. 'And foreign everywhere I go.'

With one desultory gesture I dismiss an uncongenial conversation.

'I'm tired of romance,' I overhear my companion saying.

'But without love, life's an uphill climb,' my sister muses.

Now, as I drink manzanilla, I see you in my glass. Perhaps I haven't thought of you as yet, left you behind with other things in London. Finger dipped in ink of manzanilla, I bring you into being from your place of absence, think of writing you into this narrative. (Like me, I remember, you can't swim.)

Why do we see yesterday as shadow, tell me, call memory a haunting? Echoed crooked smiles, linked fingers can thrill, become a sudden presence. Should I write: sometimes I think of you and wonder if you really happened, on occasions wish you were here to taste the green figs and the summer wine – or remind you of an evening's words that spiralled from life's work into euphoria, an empty bottle's cork I kept at dawn, some other things you left behind?

7th Extract from Refika's Notebook

'You could just come with me and forget all this,' Death says. He would write my name in pomegranate seeds, 'I love you' in cocaine. Roses and razor blades are his idea of romance. Death knows how to seduce. They are talking about love now. I turn away from him, to the living.

'I am tired of romance,' I say.

8th Postcard from Umair

At midnight we sit on the patio. My sister smokes a cigarillo, I sip brandy poured on ice. A little lizard, startled, runs up the wall. The smell I remember from Sevilla fills the air, from a bush behind my left elbow.

'Jasmine,' my sister says.

(I must remember this, to tell you: there's no frangipani here, that makes it less like Karachi.)

Now it's nearly two. My companion has retired to her room, her separate thoughts. (She wanted to visit the Alhambra. Short of time, we couldn't make it.)

Too often I treat friends like lovers, lovers as friends, give children the attention owed to adults. But friendship's all that matters. I have no time left for love. (One night – November, and the moon was full – you told me we had nowhere left to go. For a while I'd dreamt that we might travel on. It doesn't matter any more.)

My sister knows all this. I need to tell her nothing. We sit alone together. The sky hangs dark and low. We continue to talk, of small, of necessary things.

'The frangipani tree I planted will be in full flower the next time you're here ...' my sister breaks her sentence. Her eyes are very blue.

8th Extract from Refika's Notebook

The moon is full tonight. I watch her fanning herself with the palms from my bed. I lull myself to sleep by imagining I am walking barefoot through the red palace that is a pearl set in emeralds, the walls are made of a calligraphy of smoke, decorated with arabesques of remembered gestures, the fountains recite poems, the pools reflect the inky sky. But I know I'll dream again of motorways.

9th Postcard from Umair

Eyes shut, I breathe in, lost colours found again: jasmine white, fig green, hibiscus red and something new, unnamed: purple, perhaps.

The fan hums overhead. I recall one mad night's crossing, and a morning salutation: parted lips brush mine four times, and then - an afterthought? - a fifth. How should I name so accidental an exchange: inconsequence, or parting gift? What would you say?

Next door, my companion turns the tap on. What, I wonder, woke her? By my pillow, in a vase beside a jug of sparkling spring water, a twig of orange bougainvillea leans on jasmine. Like yesterday, it has no shadow and no smell.

9th Extract from Refika's Notebook

He takes me by the hand. We walk past the barking dogs, the white mare in the tall grass, down the avenue of cypresses, out of the gates, down the winding backstreets of the old town, to the edge of the land where the sea begins. And I take off my clothes and I take off my name and I swim off the page.

Refika's notes are by Alev Adil.

The Tree at the Limit

The woman, brown-haired, fine lines around brown eyes in a face that's smiled a lot. Brush in hand, body in a stained painter's smock, turning away from the window. Tree shapes through the glass: branches outlined against a grey afternoon sky. Bare branches of tall trees. At the lower left corner you sense the presence of a canvas you can't see. The colours are mild, like the back of a fallen leaf.

That's the first miniature.

~

In the second painting, the same scene, with a slight shift to the left. You see the large canvas she's been painting. It's a seascape. Glinting water, platinum on blue; perhaps an estuary. Boats with red-and-white striped sails.

There's a slight smile on her face.

~

The third painting is of a window. You see the sea through white gauze curtains.

The first two miniatures are called '*Marya, Painting*'.

The third is called '*Boats in Karachi*'.

~

The exhibition takes place in an old palace by the sea. From one of the windows, you see a scene similar to the one depicted in the painting.

~

From the exhibition catalogue:

Marya Mahmud was born in Rome in 1917. She studied art privately. She met the historian Mazhar Mahmud in 1936, probably in Paris or Berlin. They were married in a Muslim ceremony a few months later and travelled all over India during the last years of the Raj. Marya began to paint scenes as she saw them. Mahmud was an ardent nationalist and Marya, an anti-Fascist in her native country, matched his fervour in her adopted land. In 1946, a year before Independence, they moved to Lahore, where, under the influence of Chughtai, she began to paint scenes from legends and from history. In 1947, the Mahmuds moved to Karachi where Marya entered the most prolific period of her painting. In 1959 the Mahmuds left Karachi for Rome, and then moved to London.

~

The fourth miniature is of a woman's naked back; the canvas cuts her figure off just below her hips. She's lifting her hair off her neck with one hand; the other hand holds up a mirror. She's obviously balancing on one foot, as the other is raised, its heel grazing a buttock. You can see her profile in shadow. It's the woman from the tree paintings.

Through the window, the sea's a deep blue field, even though it's night. You can see a white waxing moon in the night sky. Stars are reflected in the waves. They look like yellow fish.

In the fifth, again a slight shift in perspective: seascape, window, woman and a canvas in view. It's a painting of the woman taking a pause from painting trees.

The two paintings are called '*Missing the Sea 1*' and '*Missing the Sea 2*'.

~

Between two sequences of paintings there are walls, festooned with photographs. Marya, young, before she changed her name; she was still called Maria Maddalena Serra. Marya on her wedding day with her husband, both in traditional regalia. Marya, in some Indian city, in a sari. Marya painting, cooking, on a bicycle, in a march, at a reception, meeting the Shah of Iran, meeting Nasser, Nehru. Marya, older, in Europe. There are photographs of the houses Marya lived in: Karachi, Rome, London, Cambridge.

~

From a review of the exhibition:

Marya's Oxford-educated husband, renowned historian Mazhar Mahmud, wrote a controversial book in 1959. It was called Aspects of Myth and Legend in Islamic Society. *In it he questioned the literal existence of angels, saying the Quranic word for angels didn't denote supernatural creatures with wings but only spiritual impulses transmitted to man from divine sources. The iconography of angels in later Islam was inherited from the churches and from Zoroastrian sources.*

Lucifer too: in the Holy Book he was a jinn who refused to bow to the newborn Adam, and was exiled from the Kingdom. But as he left he asked God to let him tempt mankind and give them the test of faith. Thus in some medieval legends and poems the Devil becomes God's faithful creature, an angel fallen to earth to punish him for the sin of pride, whose mission is to sift bad men from good and select the best for God. In some of the great poet Iqbal's poems, Lucifer is both adversary and admirer. But in the

Book the Devil is not the Great Enemy: he's only a whisperer and a tempter, a creature of fire, not of the light that angels are made of; a character with no power of his own and possessed of only the power that men invest in him.

~

'Papa left Karachi in '61 and Mamma went with him,' their son says, in an Italian documentary made to commemorate the artist's centenary. It's showing on a monitor with earphones appended. 'Papa felt the climate wasn't right for his book and there were rumblings from the orthodox parties. In those more tolerant times it was only a frisson, but he knew he'd overstepped the mark when a critic from the other side accused him of denying the power of angels. He was told he was being transferred to a "hardship" posting in the Gulf and he thought the time had come to work abroad. He wanted to carry out his research freely. They went together to Rome, where he worked on his book on the martyred mystic Hallaj, whom some called a heretic. When an offer came to teach in England, he left his government job and they set off for England. He would never have called himself an exile, but he thought he couldn't write the kind of books he wanted to; so he was, in a way, in self-exile. But he felt at home anywhere near a vast library, a group of intelligent students, a colleague or two to talk to; and in Cambridge he had a Fellowship and his old friend Dr Giles Hollis with whom he was going to write a book about forgotten heretics and schismatic Sufi sects. Mamma wasn't happy away from Karachi. She painted rarely and when she started to paint again her work was so bleak.'

~

The sky through the window is misty. Two treetops rise above the haze, in a violet space of sky: one's tall, the other shorter. No leaves on either. It's a winter scene. The frames of the windows are heavy, dark; painted with more detail than the mist, the haze, the treetops, the branches. The miniature is called '*The Library Window: Cambridge*'. There is no date.

'Reminds me of a pair of figurines I had on top of my TV in New York,' someone says. 'A god and a goddess. He was really tall and she was little like that tree. I think they were from Bali. Then you know I came back from holiday and found one of them gone? The little one, the lady! Obviously the cleaner just dropped it and swept it away!'

~

Scorpions in the desert sand. Cactus trees in an empty city street. Strange-shaped skulls, bones on empty beaches. A purple-skinned woman with three heads and three star-nippled breasts. A blonde androgyne dancing with a dinner-jacketed skeleton. A woman, naked, staring at a long, wild cat with a humanoid face.

Charcoal sketches. Paintings blanched of colour. These are the paintings from England that she's best known for today.

~

'But who has curated the exhibition,' someone asks in a shrill tone as they move from the stark surreal canvases to jauntily coloured pictures of folk figures from the fifties: 'Why isn't it chronological? Surely these are earlier pictures?'

'It's thematic and generic,' her companion says. 'Can't you see? These are Marya's watercolours.'

~

A deft, lightly coloured sketch of a man kneeling, his bleeding head held in his hands. In the background, hazy figures of a throng. It's called '*The Stoning of the Heretic, 1960*'. You can recognise a resemblance to her husband's features in the man's, particularly his aquiline nose, but maybe that's just the eye's imaginative licence.

~

'Papa and Mamma had never officially separated,' her daughter says.'He just began to grow away from her. He spent time in Iraq, and time in the States with Dr Hollis. Mamma would take the ship to Karachi and spend months here. I was teaching art at a girls' school and then I married and got pregnant. My brother Murtaza was working in Canada. The old house in Clifton with its view of the sea was rented out and she didn't like PECHS, the neighbourhood where I lived. Too far away from the sea! Then Papa followed Hollis to Columbia on a year's research trip and she just lingered on in the Cambridge flat, painting those desolate scenes.

'But then when my second child was on the way, she said she wanted to move back to Karachi for at least a year. She said that, as she stood on a railway platform waiting for the London train, she'd seen a falling leaf whirl by – it fell at her feet, a dead thing, all withered and crumpled, and she knew she couldn't take another cold season. Though she hated flying, she took a plane back to Karachi in a matter of days. She took calligraphy lessons and held drawing classes at home. She attended exhibitions but mostly stayed away from Karachi's other painters. Later, she taught art and French at a mixed school, and later still she worked at the university. She moved back to the Clifton house and often went for long walks, collected sea shells. My brother moved back to Pakistan in '63 and Mamma went with cultural delegations to China,

Central Asia and Egypt but she never stayed away from Karachi for any length of time.'

~

Through the library window, you see snowflakes, whirling: but look again and they're interspersed with leaves. Or they might all be leaves. The snow on the ground is a carpet of leaves.

Look again and the leaves seem to be tossed on the waves of a turbulent sea. There's a near-absence of colour that intensifies the greyish white of sky, the deep brown of trunks, the silver white of flake and leaf carpet and sea.

In the catalogue there's a detailed enlargement of a leaf.

The miniature is called '*The Tree at the Limit*'.

~

From the exhibition catalogue:

The miniature alludes to the legend of Sidrat-ul-Muntaha, the tree in paradise that marks the limit. It is said to bear as many leaves as there are people in the world. Each leaf bears the letters of a name. In the middle of the month of Shaban, the eighth month of the year, the tree shakes and sheds the leaves on which are written the names of those who will die in the coming year.

~

The exhibition opened on Marya's ninetieth birthday. She will not attend in her wheelchair, but there's a message she's recorded on film.

It's November 2007. There's a slight breeze and the sea is calm.

~

'The strange thing is that Mamma made that picture before he died in '64,' her son says in the documentary. 'He was in Iraq, with Hollis; he'd promised to come to Karachi from Iran after visiting Baghdad, Basra and a couple of places in Azerbaijan. No one knows where they were going, or why the plane crashed in Baluchistan. There were stories of sabotage and spying but there's no likely truth to any of them. The strange thing is that Mamma made that picture as if she knew ...'

~

The last miniature in the exhibition is also the first example of Marya's new phase: a piece of calligraphy. A leaf seen through glass, framed by a window, a retake of the leaf detail you saw earlier, but painted in a dense gold. Look carefully and its veins are composed of Arabic letters. The catalogue tells you they spell her husband's name.

The painting is called '*A Leaf*'. It's on the cover of the catalogue.

The Man from Beni Mora

Desert, white sand rippling, reddish sky. A figure, on a white horse, head wrapped in a scarf and covered in a hat, wearing a random assortment of Western clothes: boots, jodhpurs, a short jacket. As it comes closer, we see it's probably a very young man or a boy.

Then, from the distance, a number of horses, ridden by men in long robes. The first figure pulls out a gun and shoots. There's a round of gunfire, one of the horsemen falls, and the first figure's horse is wounded.

Another robed figure approaches, and shoots in the air: his shots might sound a code. As the other riders disperse, we see him: he's tall, beardless, frowning.

He gets off his horse, goes to the first figure who's lying in the sand, unconscious, wounded perhaps.

He takes a flask from his hip, splashes water on the recumbent boy's face, then lifts the boy's head and shoulders in his arms. We see the boy's features; not a boy after all, but a pretty young woman in her twenties, with narrow long eyes and an upturned nose.

– Ruby?

He's shaking her.

She wakes up, in a big white bed, switches the lamp on.

– What time is it?

– Six. You should be going soon. You seemed restless in your sleep. You called out my name.

– I dreamt we were in Beni Mora again. They were chasing me. And then you came ...

~

We follow her to her car as she drives through city streets to a hospital we recognise on the edges of Belgravia. As the titles come up on screen, she enters the hospital. We follow her to her office, see her name on the door. Dr Rubina Hasan.

Umair recognises the actress, Alina Murad: she's also credited as the producer. She's known for her versatility, plays traditional roles as well as transgressive parts. She's said to have been a belly dancer somewhere in the Gulf before she took to acting.

The serial is titled *Ghazali.*

Pause

– Professor Umair Omar?

– Yes.

– The London Library. We're holding two of the books you asked for. Margaret Smith's biography of Algazzaly, and the Montgomery Watt study.

– I'll be there to pick them up this afternoon by five.

– Late hours today. We're open till half past seven.

Episode

The interior of a tent. She's sitting up in bed, reading. He comes in. Tall, broad shoulders, slight stoop; in his mid- to late thirties, perhaps. He has reddish hair and hazel eyes.

– Why are you keeping me here? Why did you kidnap me? When are we going back to Beni Mora?

– You're not well enough to travel yet. And I didn't kidnap you. I rescued you. What were you doing riding in the wilderness alone after sunset?

– That's hardly your business. Can I have another book to read? I've finished the one you brought me.

– She hands it to him. We see the pale yellow cover, the bold red letters of its title: *The Rise and Fall of Islamic Thought*, by Ahmed Naseem Ghazali.

He sits down on a chair near the entrance of the tent.

– I have the book he wrote about travelling with the Tuareg. It was his doctoral dissertation.

– He's an excellent writer. Travelogues, philosophy, history ...

– He's not bad. Tends to superficiality.

– I wouldn't say you were the best judge. But when are you getting me out of here?

– The doctor says you're still in shock. I'm going to Beni Mora today. When I come back in three days I'll take you there.

Pause

Why Beni Mora? Umair thinks. Is it even a real place? He does a search on his mobile and remembers where he's seen it before: in that old orientalist chestnut, *The Garden of Allah*, starring Marlene Dietrich. He remembers the film was taken from a novel. What are they doing here, the producer, the scriptwriter, reproducing an orientalist chestnut? The titles say the book is 'inspired by the novel of the same name', but he's never heard of an Urdu novel called *Ghazali*, nor of the writer, a woman. He turns to his book, but leaves the television on. There's a long scene he's aware of, with the young woman leaving her bed, stealing a horse, riding across the desert. He wonders if the film crew really went to North Africa, or whether they shot the film in Sindh or Balochistan. The exteriors are impressive: the whites and reds, the sky, sand and date palms of the opening have given way now to rock, scrub, barren pathways. The silent scene ends in a hill town that looks authentic: white buildings, winding lanes. Digital technology, he thinks. To recreate the past. Must be set in the fifties.

Episode

Now she's in a hotel ballroom, in a long white gown. With a girl who looks European. The people around her are speaking French.

– We're going to meet Dr Ghazali, Ruby. The hotel manager said he was here and asked if we would join him for dinner. I said we'd be delighted if instead he'd join us.

– I don't know if it's a good idea to meet a writer you've read; he's probably very old and a bore.

– Oh, I hear he's a fascinating man. The French authorities don't like him. He spreads subversion among the natives, rebellion ...

He approaches, in a dinner jacket, joins them at their table, that man we know from the desert.

– Oh, Miss Warburton. I know Miss Hasan. We've met. I rescued her from the desert bandits on the outskirts of Beni Mora. (He sneers.)

– Dr Rubina Hasan. She's a surgeon, the European girl says. I told her not to ride alone but she's a headstrong girl.

– I didn't know who he was, though. Why didn't you tell me?

– Oh, I didn't want to spoil your pleasure in reading ...

The period atmosphere of the film is effective because it's created impressionistically. You, the viewer, are in the past, which could be the forties or the fifties, even has touches of the sixties; but it's also timeless. Umair recognises the actor playing Ghazali. Babur Awan. One of the best known in Karachi. Earlier he was confused by the dyed hair, the greenish lenses.

– Why did you run away?

– You were keeping me against my will ... I knew I could get back alone to Beni Mora.

– You didn't get back alone. You were being followed by my men. It wasn't safe for you to ride alone.

Umair has noticed now that they deliver their lines in a mannered way that moves from the naturalistic mode of television drama to something measured, almost staccato, akin to declamation or chanting. He thinks the lines have been written in blank verse, to scan.

– Do you spend much time in England, Dr Ghazali?

– I have a house there in Surrey. That's where I'm planning to write my book about Beni Mora. My grandfather left it to me. My mother was English.

Pause

Umair wakes up on the sofa. He's been trying to write the first chapter of his memoir, which is meant to be a recollection of a happy youth and a sad-sweet love affair. He had fallen asleep reading a rather turgid translation of *The Alchemy of Happiness* online. The serial's on again, he remembers. It's on every night of the week, from two to three, often too late for him to watch, but he's become addicted. He wonders why the hero has been named after Ghazali; we know he's a polymath, but nothing else seems to link him to a theologian and a mystic. Let's see, he thinks, and switches on to watch.

Episode

In the recap that flashes on the screen, we see Rubina and Ghazali, both in Western wedding dress, outside a building that announces its function with a big sign: THE ISLAMIC CENTRE.

Then they're in an English country garden, in winter clothes. In the backdrop there's a big house, the kind of mansion that heritage TV and Bollywood delight in. The grounds are covered with snow; the lake is icy.

Ghazali is talking:

– I first went there when I was very young. I studied Arabic in Oxford. In Beni Mora I set up schools and taught children to read. One day someone asked me to lead a congregation in prayer because they think all educated men are religious scholars and though I'd learnt it all as a boy, I found to my shame I'd forgotten.

It was then that I first became close to my maker whom I'd always taken for granted and began to pray as often as I could, sometimes more than five times a day. I came back and did my doctorate in Islamic studies, travelled to Cairo ...

– Yes, I loved Beni Mora, Rubina is saying. You know my father sent me here to England when I was very young, barely fourteen, and I haven't been back to Lahore since. I have memories of home, but Beni Mora was nothing like what I remember. I had never seen the desert before, yet some part of me felt as if I had come to a place that I knew, where I may even once have belonged. I loved the simplicity of the people and even more I loved the boundlessness of sand and sky. Sometimes in those absences I felt I was alone in the presence of something greater than I was, though I don't believe in anything but absence ...

– Do you know they say reason never leads you to faith? Your heart does. It comes like a light that enters you. Look around you, Rubina, look at these gardens that are frozen over, the leaves gone from the trees, the birds flown south ... they'll be back, and then they'll be gone again. Can this happen without an order in our world, and someone who creates that order so that nothing varies, even change is changeless ... You know they say that God is the greatest artist? The world is beautiful, Rubina, and that beauty comes from Him.

Ghazali's monologue continues, lyrical, hypnotic. Umair feels he's heard the words before, and thinks, at first, that they might have been paraphrased from the Quran. He reflects on the beauty of Urdu, of its sounds that, like its letters, reach his eyes, reach something in his inner ear that the other languages he knows don't reach. Indian syntax, Persian images, Arabic alphabet, terms he doesn't always understand. He remembers how a teacher once told him that Persian was tactile and descriptive but Arabic excelled in abstract contextual terms. If Persian praises God's beauty (jamal), he thinks, then Arabic evokes His splendour (jalal). The thought of beauty reminds him of Ghazali's namesake and he wonders whether these words are borrowed from the original Ghazali's. ('Ghazali,' Margaret Smith wrote, 'thinks of plants and flowers not only as things of beauty and a source of keen delight to every lover of nature, but also as displaying the wisdom and loving kindness of God, Who has given the fruit its rind so that it may be protected from the birds.') And as Ghazali's onscreen namesake intones his encomium, the seasons around him change: leaves appear on the trees, pears blossom. We are in an English spring garden. Swans glide on the pale surface of the still lake. The foliage of summer surrounds them. Then the leaves falling, red, olive and burnt gold. Colours explode on film like fireworks, nearly artificial, but recognisably those of the world around us. Once again Umair suspects the use of digital technology. Ghazali and Rubina walk through these changing landscapes of a virtual world, their clothes changing with the seasons. They're holding hands, laughing. Umair thinks that the changes indicate the passing of time in the film, but he's wrong: the changing seasons were Ghazali's fantasy, and suddenly we're back to winter, to Rubina's point of view.

– That's the way of nature. I'm a doctor, I believe in my work and in saving lives and serving my kind that way, that's my only mission. I don't believe in faith, or in a Creator. My father was an unbeliever and he brought me up that way. I'm amazed that an intellectual like you can believe in a first cause. I think it's just accidental collisions and a fusion of particles. You know what my dream is? To go back to the country I left behind and set up a hospital there. I'm going to do that, Ghazali, very soon ...

– And us? What about us?

– Won't you come back with me? Can't you help? As you did in Beni Mora?

Umair wants to keep on watching, but his mind is sleepily wandering. It's unusual to see a woman speaking of atheism so directly in a commercial teleplay. He's noticed that Pakistani drama serials often seem to be about religion. He's seen one in which a rich boy discovers religion to come close to the poor teacher's daughter he loves, but loses her anyway to conflict and death. He's seen one in which a Hindu refugee is drawn to Islam by the simple faith of her benefactor. He's seen one in which two headscarved women, visiting from the States, have to fight the prejudices of their chic Karachi hostesses who neither fast nor pray. Most often, the religious win, but they aren't what you'd call fundamentalists. You also see bigots, both men and women, in these plays, and they're comic when they aren't downright evil. There's a battle going on and it's difficult to draw the lines between the devout and the bigoted, male and female. The atheists, of course, are in their own enclosed world. But what's unusual is to find the heroine speaking the lines of devil's advocacy, without villainy or parody, just in normal, if scathing, tones. Alina's mildly scandalous reputation makes her even more convincing in her portrayal. Is that why she chose to produce the film? To give an atheist a voice?

When his attention returns to the play, Ghazali and Rubina, in their night clothes, are fighting wordlessly in their bedroom: he isn't sure whether he's switched the sound off, but he's too lazy to reach for the control which is lying on the floor. He looks at the subtitles instead.

– You said you wouldn't go back to work for six weeks. We've been married a fortnight. What about our plans to go back to Beni Mora?

– You knew who I was when you married me. You knew you were marrying a doctor.

Ghazali flings some clothes into a suitcase, walks to the hall where he pulls on an overcoat which he retrieves from a coat rack, puts on shoes and goes out into the night. Then we see a vintage car driving through foggy streets. It draws up at the Savoy Hotel. We watch Ghazali descend. Umair had thought there'd be an accident. That Rubina would rush to wounded Ghazali's bedside and there'd be a reconciliation.

Montage

Still and moving images, in colour and in sepia.

Ghazali, in Beni Mora, teaching children.

Rubina, giving birth. (That's a long, silent scene.)

Ghazali in the jungle, on safari. (He has a gun, but remember the story is set in pre-conservation times, when even a good man's allowed to hunt; or maybe he's culling.)

Rubina in Karachi, building a hospital in a village.

Ghazali, in Zulu territories, teaching adults, writing English letters on a blackboard.

Documentary footage in black and white (is it genuine?) of a hospital being inaugurated by a ribbon-cutting dignitary in a long coat and a tall woolly hat.

Rubina, with her son, walking by the sea, playing ball.

Ghazali, writing. A series of books on travel, history and time. Their phantom covers flash on the screen and we wonder at his rate of production.

Ghazali's voice over the virtual images of book covers. Oddly enough, in English.

– Dearest love – you may wonder that I still call you that, but the pain you caused me made me understand that there's more to life than beauty, and I'm back to doing what I do best. I feel you found your way to what you believed in. I hear you are a dedicated doctor and your hospital is thriving. You achieved what I never could; I'm just a scribe, and do what little I can, but that's the road I know, travelling, teaching and writing about what I see and the history of the places I visit. Then I travel on. Each one of us on the path we found that suited us best, you with your science and me with my wandering search. I'm back in Beni Mora. I don't know how long I'll stay. I want to go to Andalusia next; it's so long since I wrote my book about it. But I'm tired and a little ill and for now Beni Mora is where I'll rest.

Rubina, on a balcony in an old villa overlooking the sea in Karachi's Clifton, feeding pigeons. She sits down, takes the letter from a silver tray, reads it; she's about to tear it up, then changes her mind.

Pause

Umair goes away for two weeks, to Italy, Scotland, and Yorkshire. He's given up his memoir, given up reading Ghazali, but he has been thinking about the serial; he ordered the novel the film derived from, but when it arrived from Pakistan he saw they'd sent the wrong book, and anyway the scriptwriters in Pakistan tend to adapt quite freely from the novels they dramatise so they'll have changed it all, particularly the sequence of events. But he wants to know what happens to Rubina, to Ghazali, though he knows that like life the endings of Pakistani serials can be inconclusive, even abrupt.

It's not showing late at night any more, and he can't trace a change of time on the Sky menu. But he knows that the last one he saw can't have been the final episode.

Then one night he decides to try on YouTube. Nothing. He finds two episodes on a TV website, both of which say 'final', but he doesn't know whether that means the serial has ended, or just that the episode online is the last one shown. He downloads the first one.

Final Episode 1

– Headache. Headache.

The child was wailing all night.

He's in a hospital bed now, in a private room.

Meningitis. He might not survive.

Help.

He's all I have.

– Only prayer will help, the nurses say.

Delirium.

She's sitting beside the boy's bed. His breathing is ragged.

Ghazali has sent her his latest book. *Prayer in Islam: Selected Translations.*

Almost as a reflex action, she brought it with her. She opens it.

– You win, Ghazali. I'm asking for help. You could say I'm praying. For my son who is also yours.

She hears his echoing voice as she reads:

– God is the light of the skies and of the earth. The semblance of His light is that of a niche in which is a lamp, the lamp within a glass, the glass is a glittering star as it were, lit with the oil of a blessed tree, the olive, neither of the east nor of the west, whose oil appears to light up even though fire touches it not, – light upon light. God guides to His light whom he will.

– I don't know who You are or if You or Your light exist, but tonight I'm prepared to pray to You to save my child.

She covers her head with her shawl and repeats the words that might bring back the light.

Final Episode 2

You are in Beni Mora, where you almost always seem to find yourself after dark. The sand, dotted with distant date palms, stretches away from you, towards the horizon, seeming to slip away, from under your feet. You're calling. You know your child was sleeping safely beside you when you last opened your eyes. But now he isn't there. You're barefoot and the sand burns the soles of your feet. You're calling, in the dark. Then, in the distance, the man in white. You know you've been there before, in your dreams, but you can't wake yourself up this time. The child is beside the man, holding his hand. Who are you, you call, do I know your name, tell me your name ...

He stretches out his hand to you.

– Ghazali?

You wake up. You go to the window: you can see the faint first shimmer of light on the water and you know the night is almost over.

The Swan's Wife

1

I once knew a woman who loved a swan. She loved all swans, and geese and ducks and waterhens too, but most of all she loved a swan she called Satin. On Sundays, we went to the park to feed the birds that nested among the rushes beside the lake. They'd come running after us and pluck at our calves with their beaks. Satin would wait until she'd fed the rest, and then glide up to her with his mate. She would feed him pellets of bread she'd moistened in her mouth, and often he'd follow her like a pet, as his mate hopped along behind.

Maia – that was her name – and I lived on different sides of the park, she by the western gate, and I by the south. In summer, the park was full of teenagers cavorting, boating, jumping into the lake. Elderly couples strolled in the rose garden, the men with their bellies hanging out of their open shirts over their Bermuda shorts, their wives in thin shifts with their bare arms freckling and their faces flushed. There was a brass band, and a bandstand, with chairs for hire and people selling ice cream.

Sometimes the boys on their roller skates would bully the birds. They'd tempt them with scraps of food; when the birds came over, the boys would chase them with sticks and stones. And then the birds would show how strong they were. There was an urban legend about a goose that had attacked a boy with beak and claw and nearly plucked his eye out. But the swans kept to the water, their nests and their own company, and only Satin ever left the lake.

In the middle of the park was a grand house that had once belonged to a rich merchant who had brought back a fortune from India. It was filled with objects he had acquired on his travels; you could see them twice a week for the price of a ticket, but apart from groups of school children, people barely bothered to visit the house.

As you approached it, the house seemed to be right in the middle of the lake, but that was an illusion – it was built on a piece of land that jutted into the water. They said the merchant had filled the lake with waterbirds, so he could look out at them from one of the house's many windows.

Sometimes, when I walked by the water alone, I'd remember the artificial lake I'd read about in a book of old swan tales that I'd been given as a present many years ago. The lake was made by the servants of a king called Karan, who wanted it to be the meeting place of all the birds in the world. At that time, the swans had their own kingdom far away in Lake Manasa, in the mountains near Tibet. King Karan had heard of Lake Manasa, and dreamt that his lake should rival it in beauty. In summer, the young swans of Manasa would fly overhead and take home reports of this clear lake that rivalled theirs, with fish of every colour in its depths and flowers of every colour on its margins. They'd swoop down to drink, but they would never linger: they fed only on freshwater pearls, and there were no pearls on the bed of the artificial lake. I looked for the book on my shelf, but I'd probably lost it long ago, or left it behind somewhere when I outgrew fairy tales and other childish things.

2

Maia's parents were from a Balkan province that had changed hands and name after World War II. Her father survived the mayhem, but some years after she was born, he defected with his wife and his two children. They moved to London via Paris, as refugees. Maia didn't remember her Balkan childhood at all.

At school she wasn't terribly good at her studies, but she had a flair for languages, music and dance. She was very pretty too, with long, black hair and almond eyes that changed colour from brown to green depending on the light. When she was fourteen, her mother put her in stage school. At seventeen, she joined a troupe of dancers and played some minor roles on television, and even a bit part in a Bond movie, but she wasn't suited to that life, she said. ('Too many foul old men with sweaty hands.') At eighteen, she met an actor and moved in with him. But he was violent and possessive; when he was out of work, which was often, he'd clean flats for a living. She thought he was seeing other women. One night she ran away and went back home to her parents.

I'd moved to live near the park late in the winter of '78, in my twenty-third year. I'd met Maia a few times, a year or two before that; she had once slept on my sister Sasha's sofa for a week, in Sasha's Chelsea flat. But we'd become friends one afternoon when I was walking by the lake and thinking about my life. She called out my name from behind – she remembered my name, though she said it oddly – and we sat down on a bench in the sick February sunshine to talk. She'd moved to a new garden flat a minute's walk away from the park. Her life, she said, was going better: she'd got a job as a buyer in a fashion company, and was designing clothes as well. I worked in a bank and hated my job. It all poured out as we spoke.

We exchanged numbers and started to meet. On Saturdays, we walked by the lake and fed the swans and often in the evenings we would stroll down High Street and eat a pizza or a plate of spaghetti.

Then spring came and she went to Milan for a show. I was alone and had almost no friends in London. Just after my twenty-third birthday in April, I decided to leave the bank and apply to go back to university.

For some months I felt Maia was avoiding me. But then, that summer before I went back to my studies, she started to call again and we met often. I would tell her about the girl I was seeing; she'd talk about the man she'd fallen in love with. He was about ten years older; a count, she said, from a Balkan state, like the one she came from.

'He walked into the store one day and my manager told me to help him,' she said. 'He bought the most expensive dresses in the store – for his sister, he said – and the day after I received, gift-wrapped, the one I liked the best, with a bunch of roses and an invitation for a glass of champagne.'

She'd been apprehensive at first – she'd met many, many men who only wanted a brief fling – but he dropped her home and asked to see her again later in the week.

And then they'd seen each other again, and again.

'He wants to marry me,' she said, and showed me her ruby ring. 'Pre-engagement. He's very rich.' And then, with a grimace: 'My mother approves. She says I won't find another man who'll look after me the way he will.'

That's what had been happening to her while I was leaving my job.

We spent long days in the park that summer – Saturdays, Sundays – feeding the birds, walking, climbing trees, singing to each other, or just lying silently on the grass, sharing cigarettes.

In October, I was back at university, studying languages. I was singing again too, with an acoustic folk group I'd found at college.

In the autumn evenings, if we met after a day's work, we'd either eat something together at a restaurant – a pizza or a plate of pasta – or go back to her flat for something exquisitely simple she'd cooked. But often we'd leave each other on a street corner, and be off to our other pursuits: she to her nightclubs and five-star restaurants, and I with my new acquaintances to their student hangouts. Just as often I'd go to a concert or a film on my own, or home to an evening alone with a book.

3

Maia soon found out that Maximilian, her lover, was married and waiting for a divorce.

'I'm not making any commitments till his decree is final,' she said.

It was November, and we had our overcoats on. We were striding rather than strolling.

She'd tried to break up with him after one of their champagne-fuelled nights, and he'd gone away, but he'd rung her bell later, quite drunk. ('He's fond of gin and of cognac.')

'He swears he'll kill himself if I leave him,' she told me as we sat down on a bench by the lake and lit cigarettes.

So the fairy-tale ending wasn't about to be staged yet.

'Another bloody freak,' I said. 'Why do you always attract freaks?'

(I was retaliating to a comment she'd made once, when she met a Spanish friend of mine: 'Is she an au pair?' And when I said she was studying philosophy, she said, 'Why do you always date such *common* girls?')

'Max is not violent,' she said. 'Never ever!'

4

In winter, the park was almost empty after midday. But Maia liked to go there in all seasons: summer, autumn and winter, in sunshine and even in snow. Once when I hadn't seen her for some weeks, she dragged me out on a Saturday afternoon in early January. It had snowed so hard that the lake had frozen over. She was looking for Satin, but couldn't find him.

'He's probably flown to sunnier shores,' I said.

But she knew he'd be there.

And then we heard his call.

He was on the island in the lake, where he had his nest, but when she called out to him, he wouldn't come over.

'He's wounded,' she said. 'I know. He's hurt his wing. Or a foot.'

(Was he afraid of the ice? If so, why couldn't he fly? Had his wings been clipped?)

Maia threw off her fur coat, flung it on the frost-spangled grass, and set off across the glittering ice floor.

(And I'd heard since I was very young that swans never parted from their mates. So where had Satin's mate gone, leaving him stranded?)

'Satin, O Satin, come on boy, come to Maia ...'

She slipped as soon as she stepped on the ice. I grabbed her before she fell. She sat down on a bench, pulled off her boots and her stockings, and set off again, barefoot, to cross the water. I heard Satin crying. Maia shrieked when her bare foot touched its frozen surface.

'You'll fall,' I said. 'The ice will crack.'

She said: 'There were kids skating on the lake earlier. The ice won't give way.'

And I don't remember the ice cracking or her falling or whether she ever got to the island. But I do remember her characteristically rambling story about wardens and vets and, yes, a swan hospital in Richmond, and three men struggling to get poor Satin on a boat and then into their van. He'd broken a foot and would have to be off the lake for quite a while.

I must have told her then about the day the famine came to the swans of Lake Manasa.

The swans, the story said, had eaten all the pearls in the lake. Then the pair that were the bravest among them flew off in search of fresh pearls. They flew over all the world's lakes, but were too proud to stop for food and water. One day, they flew over a lake that was surrounded by pearls that gleamed on the petals of the flowers and on the grass like dewdrops. The male swan swooped down to pick up the pearls: tired, he set his feet on the grass, but soon he found his silver left foot was caught in a trap concealed in a net into which the pearls had been woven.

King Karan, who had been watching the swans from a terrace, approached and said to the swan in the trap: 'Eat, swan, eat the pearls I laid out for you! Eat and I'll let you go.'

And the swan replied: 'Never! You have tricked me.'

Karan cried: 'Why will you not eat? Have I not made a lake for you that rivals Manasa in beauty? And am I not generous? Have I not laid seed pearls around it for you and your army of swans to feed on?'

Then the swan's wife said from her perch in the air: 'Kings do not imprison the innocent. Kings do not war against women.'

In one version, the swan's wife flew away to look for help; in another, the king's men shot her down with a golden arrow. In a third telling, the swan didn't even have a wife; the one who came to rescue him from King Karan was his intrepid friend.

5

I wasn't serious about anyone I'd met; I'd had flings too, but mostly I was happy enough to study and listen to music when I was on my own. And I had Maia. Max only visited for short periods – he'd stay in a smart boutique hotel in Kensington where he seemed to have a permanent reservation, see her for dinner or drop in at her flat, and always bring her gifts: jewels, furs, gowns. Much of the time Maia was alone and we spent our best times together. More than once I got the feeling she didn't really care when Max failed to turn up. Once the first tide of joy subsided, the old pain came back – her first lover had left her with scars of betrayal that would never heal.

Over the spring we became closer and closer,

almost like twins. I felt she enjoyed talking about love, or dreaming of it, more than she enjoyed living it. (Both of us liked to be liked, but once we'd got the object of our affection, we were less interested and often longed to escape the possessiveness of our lovers.)

Like all dreamers, she was very unpunctual, as she sat for hours in front of the mirror, though I don't think it was herself she was looking at. She loved eating and cooking (and like most of us who do, she often complained of indigestion and stomach ailments). Once when she was cooking for me at her place – a chicken with aromatic herbs, and a dish of pilaff with nuts and raisins – Max rang and said he'd join us for dinner, because a meeting of his had been cancelled. He was a dark-haired man of medium height, with a long nose and very black eyes. He had a slow, hoarse voice and affected mannerisms and didn't seem to be enjoying his food very much. I was waiting to make my getaway when he suggested we should all go to a nightclub called the Saddle Room. I watched while they danced away the night. It was the first time I'd seen him; I hoped it would be the last.

For a woman who loved birds so much and couldn't bear to see a stray dog or cat on a street corner in some southern city, Maia was unconcerned about the hunting down of wild animals. So she'd put a stuffed tiger in her sitting room to shock all her eco-conscious friends. She took a photograph of me embracing the tiger and giggled because it actually wasn't stuffed at all; it was a mere fake. She loved taking photographs and she loved her Polaroid camera. She took pictures of me: singing, dancing, and posing in every angle one evening when the rain was coming down hard outside. Then she disappeared into her bedroom, and emerged dressed up as some long-gone Hollywood diva: Ava Gardner perhaps, her favourite. She handed over her Polaroid to me and I took pictures of her too, some out of focus, some quite good, especially one in which she looked like a captive beauty from one of those old ballads I loved to sing, with her arms around her furry black-and-golden beast, looking out with yearning eyes, dreaming that he'd be transformed into a prince.

Maia loved dancing. Once, after a drink or two of champagne, she draped a few scarves round her brassiere and tucked one into her panties, put on a record of Arabic instrumental music really loud and undulated like an Egyptian, twisting her belly and swinging her hips, and clashing the cymbals attached to her fingertips, while I lay back on the sofa and lazily kept time with my hands and my feet. Then she dragged me up to dance with her and we wriggled face-to-face, but we never let our bodies touch. She was affectionate but she didn't like being touched, and I was afraid of what the touch of her perspiring skin might unleash in me.

She loved music, but didn't really understand the dirge-like folk songs I sang. We both spoke Italian and when I was a child I'd picked up a lot of Italian big-band melodies like '*Volare*' and '*Come Prima, Piu di Prima*'. I went off and learnt the lyrics of those songs to entertain her; I belted them out to her in a fair imitation of Mario Lanza in the kitchen while she baked a cheese and spinach pie, and kept on singing in the doorway of her bathroom as she soaked in her bubble bath before we sat down to supper.

We spent a lot of time in her tiny over-furnished basement flat as autumn approached. We both worked all day; unless we met in the park just before it closed, we didn't have time to meet before dark. And since Satin hadn't come back to the lake, Maia seemed to want to walk in the park much less often. Once or twice she called out when we did go in search of him: 'Look! Satin!' But the swan we saw hadn't approached her, and she decided that it wasn't Satin after all. So we'd stay indoors together on our free afternoons.

But something or someone often came between us: her travels, my studies, her family or mine, but mostly Max. I told myself I didn't mind when Max turned up – I'd feel lonely, but I'd make the best of the time I had for myself. And I had other friends now. The closest of these was Fabi. We'd met on the way home from a university social; he'd called me several times when I'd been busy with her. Then one day I bumped into him by the French Institute where we were queueing for a concert and we sat down together. We both liked French films, Jacques Brel and Sartre. To look at, though, we were opposites: Fabi was smaller than me, he was blonde and I was dark, he was ebullient and I was quiet, he was a scientist and I was a student of humanities.

Fabi believed there was safety in numbers: he didn't bother to change girlfriends, he just waited till one or the other of them got tired of his feckless, faithless ways and dropped him, before another one appeared in his life. He liked going out and drinking beer and staying out all night; as for me, it was hard to drag me to a crowded, dark place with loud music playing, except, perhaps, on a Saturday, because I knew what it felt like to be left alone while Maia was in Rio de Janeiro and the rest of the world was drinking and dancing.

Fabi and Maia met once or twice; they didn't like each other.

6

Fall, leaves, please fall! I'd say to the trees when autumn approached. The lull at the start of November was spellbinding, but I was afraid of bare branches and wished the leaves would rain down now so that I could get used to the naked trees. By the time the leaves had begun to fall around us and squelch beneath our feet in red-and-yellow piles, I was too busy to think much about the park or Satin and the other swans on the lake. (For all I knew, they'd all flown off to Lake Manasa.) Apart from my studies, there was the work I did in an office a couple of times a week; my few leisure hours were spent with my musical friends, practising for our performances in clubs and college halls.

Maia was on and off planes every few days. I was never very clear about what sort of business took her away – she said she was attending fashion shows and buying new designs. I'd tell her she had travel fever, was happiest at airports and in hotels, and would never turn down a chance to fly. Sometimes she was away for three weeks and I wouldn't even hear from her. Or she'd call on a bad line and wake me up at dawn because she was in Hong Kong or Buenos Aires and had forgotten the time difference.

When she was in town, we'd meet just as we always had. But our relationship was enclosed in a glass bubble now. She liked to meet in West End hotel bars, and looked around her a lot as if she were afraid of spies. She'd started to bring gifts for me: shirts, ties, a watch, a lighter. She seemed restless. I felt her loneliness. Max had stopped talking about divorcing his wife; she was completely opposed to the idea of being the 'mistress', as she put it, of a married man. Now other names were appearing on her list of suitors. An ageing MP. A Saudi princeling. But all of them seemed to be spoken for. She was smoking far too much and complaining of her bad appetite and recurrent stomach cramps.

Once at the Students' Union Bar, when I got there late after seeing her, Fabi, who'd been waiting nearly an hour for me, said over his dwindling second pint: 'When that woman turns up and just crooks a little finger, you dump the lot us, and off you run. What's with you, man?'

And I realised that things really had changed between all of us. I'd fallen into a lot of Fabi's ways, going out carousing till two in the morning even on weekdays, then stumbling red-eyed out of bed to attend my classes. I'd pretend to Maia, when she remarked on the purple shadows under my eyes, that I'd been studying till late, but she knew me too well to believe that for more than a minute. 'You're burning your candle at both ends, darling ...' She'd laugh, but there was a brittle tinge to her words and to her laughter, as if I, her reliable friend, was turning into someone she could no longer lean on.

Twice in autumn I'd taken off on a whim, without telling anyone, to spend long weekends in Barcelona and Paris, and been scolded for missing lectures. The truth was that I liked it when she rang and couldn't find me. And when I came back to find that she hadn't called during those days and there was only Fabi to explain my mysterious movements, I'd be annoyed, because telling her later that I'd been away all the time that she had just didn't have the same impact as her ringing to find me gone.

I felt guilty as I spoke to Fabi now, as if I were betraying her, but I wanted clarity, and I spoke as I'd never done before.

'I'm sick of it all,' I said. 'I miss her when she leaves. Then just as I get used to her being away, she turns up, and if I can't see her, she sounds offended. She regularly breaks promises she makes. Let's go here or there on Sunday, she'll say, then on Sunday she'll be off to Timbuktu or Ulan Bator. Let's go to the sea, she'll say, but the only waters we've ever seen ourselves in together are those of the park ...'

Fabi's mind seemed to wander as he looked into the depths of his glass. And then he said, furrowing his brow: 'Who – or what – do you think pays for those gifts she gives you? What does she ask for, in return? You're not sleeping with her, are you? You need to find a girlfriend. What are you like, weird?'

He saw my face darken, I imagine. He passed me a Gitane.

'Fancy coming to Rome for Christmas?'

He knew it was my favourite city. I smiled and didn't answer.

7

Sometimes I'd dream that Maia had fallen into the lake, that she was calling out for help, calling out my name and waving, and then she was neck-deep in water, and I was standing on the icy bank, with my feet frozen, dumb and unable to move, watching her drown. I'd wake up in a cold sweat and the dream would overlay what really happened that winter day with Satin.

If by chance I wandered into the park during her absence, I'd see her walking by the lake, hear her calling to her swan. Then I'd ask myself why I was so attached to one person when the whole wide world deserved my love and attention, why I had to put up with this travesty of tenderness that imprisoned me in its tight, little iron ring.

We met in the dark Hilton bar. She was just back from Milan.

'Remember those days? How we spent day after day in the park? And how we rescued Satin ...'

There was a kind of yearning in her gestures and her words.

It was Happy Hour. We were drinking foul concoctions of vodka and Tia Maria, the sort of sweet sloppy drink Maia favoured when she wasn't drinking champagne.

'But that wasn't even a year ago. You make it sound like ten years–'

'We were so happy then. It's just that we were so happy–'

'I'm not at all unhappy now, Maia. Are you?'

'No, no, I'm always happy when I see you.'

But you haven't been happy for a while, I thought. Yes, you're happy for a moment when you see me and then you're off somewhere, in some place I can't reach.

Maia's way of seeing happiness as if it was always something that had happened yesterday made me anxious for a tomorrow round the corner. I wanted to live in the present. Other people's nostalgia made me sad. And then I'd think that though she listened cheerfully to the stories I told her, and asked whom I flirted with or even made love with, our friendship was – always had been – based on her stories. And my responses to those stories. Her travels. Her troubles. And now, along with stories, there were hopes. A home. Babies. A world that was remote from me and anything I wanted.

And what about my future? I'd take my degree and study some more for a higher one. I'd go travelling in Asia, which I hadn't seen since I left home nine years ago. And I was going to sing again. I hadn't been singing since my second year exams.

What place then would Maia have in my life? She'd marry and move on. So what was the point of thinking beyond that?

I'd never spoken to Maia about tomorrow. But sometimes she would say: 'We're going to be together forever. Never let me go.'

Come prima, piu di prima, t'amero ...

8

A lonely December Sunday. I was tired of studying and reading and even of music. I took a coach to Oxford to spend a day with my sister Sasha, who'd moved there the year before with her academic husband.

We went for a walk in the university gardens among the deer. She asked about Maia, who'd once been a friend of sorts.

'Fabi thinks I give her too much time. He doesn't believe in platonic friendships.'

'Fabi's right. This friendship's going nowhere, hmmm? Maia's involved with someone else. You'll be twenty-five in spring; you have your studies to finish next year. And weren't you planning to go back to Karachi with Dad next year? And then continue with your studies? And these expensive gifts she brings you ... have you ever given her anything in return? You don't have a job or a decent income. You study, you sing, you live the life of Riley. Maybe it's because of you that Maia isn't being able to make a decision. Now it's up to you to think of the future ...'

We turned a corner and sat down in a walled garden in which roses grew in summer. We didn't talk for a while.

Later, as we strolled by the river, I saw a single swan glide by. For the first time in months, I thought of Satin.

9

In the coach, on my way home in the winter darkness, I remembered a picture of a pair of swans in the book I'd lost. One was skimming the deep blue water, looking at the sky; the other raised her head from what seemed at first glance to be a tangled nest of thorns in the river. But if you looked again, you could see that she was in the embrace of a giant black bird, his grey beak at her throat, one black talon on her wing and the other on her white and bleeding breast, and what seemed to be water wasn't water at all, it was darkening sky. The body of the swan lay on night-dark soil. Underneath the picture was the legend: *Between you and me there is no kinship.*

They say that once a wounded crow who had flown too high in the sky fell into the swans' nest. The swan gave the hungry, tired crow refuge, but it was an ambush. The crow claimed that he had come to reclaim his mate, the swan's wife. An army of a hundred crows swooped down from above them to peck at the swan's wings and at his eyes; they chased him away from his nest at the lake's edge. The swan hovered in the air above his wife, held off by the army of crows, and the wind was his home and a cloud his nest, and he cried for his mate. (And the cry of a swan is a fearful thing.)

Seeing that swan on the lake had reminded me of the tale. But why, in the picture, was the swan looking away from the crow and from his bleeding wife? *Between you and me there is no kinship*: those were the words the swan in the story said to the crow when he offered him refuge. But the intent of the picture left me in doubt. Were those cruel words the swan's farewell to his mate?

(And the cry of a swan torn away from his mate is a fearful thing.)

10

'I'm going to be twenty-nine on the twenty-second,' she said. 'I thought I'd have a party here ... just you and me and a few friends.'

We'd finished eating our lobster; we were on our second bottle of wine.

'But you said you were going to see the Nile in winter with Max–'

'Changed my mind. That bastard hasn't done a thing about his divorce ...'

And it occurred to me that Maximilian, with his black hair and his long nose, looked just like the crow in the illustration.

'But Maia, I'm not going to be here. I'm going to Rome over the Christmas break. I'll be gone by then, before the rush begins.'

I'd only decided as we spoke that I'd be going to Rome.

For a minute I thought she was going to cry. Then she looked up and said, 'But you'll come back for the new year, won't you?'

It was going to be the start of a new decade.

'Yes,' I said. 'I'll be back to spend it with you, Maia.'

I knew that by the time I returned, things would have changed again.

She smiled. Her eyes in the candlelight were amber.

'I've been meaning to tell you. Satin's back on the lake. I saw him.'

A few months ago I'd have told her she had dreamt it all; that she'd seen some other hungry swan and decided it was her old pet who'd escaped from the wily king, the traps, the crows, the wicked boys and the swan doctors. That I didn't know a thing about the comings and goings of swans or their seasonal habits, and even if I'd ever cared, I didn't any more. But tonight I thought I'd leave her with her fancies of a big white bird preening his feathers and spreading his wings on the frozen winter lake.

I leant over the debris of dinner to kiss her cheek, but it was her mouth that met mine.

'Let me order us a cognac for the road,' I said. 'Then I should walk you home.'

Freely adapted from his original Urdu story 'Maya aur Hans' by the author.

The Entrepreneurs

'You have to try the biryani I make,' Mr Beg said as he stitched a cushion cover. 'I swear it would leave lords and princes licking their fingers, ma'am.'

Then the conversation turned to different types of biryani, and Beg probably dropped a few stitches as he prepared his imaginary feast.

Beg had arrived in London only a short while ago. He said he'd had a big furniture business in the Gulf. 'I employed several craftsmen, ma'am, and picked up all their different lingos. Then, one by one, they left for home when they'd earned enough money, some to Thailand, others to the Philippines or Indonesia. The business ground to a standstill, so I packed up and left for London.'

Lean and lanky, with grizzled hair and protruding

teeth, Beg was a talkative man. His continuous chatter was, in Mrs Meer's words, enough to wash all the wax out from one's ears.

It so happened that Mrs Meer talked about Beg's culinary expertise to several of her friends and set their taste buds tingling. One offered her kitchen for a cooking session. 'Why not come to my place, which is more spacious, and bring your lovely apricot pudding?' another suggested. A young doctor friend from Bihar said he'd make a dish of haleem; his wife vetoed the idea because serving biryani and haleem at the same meal was profligate and the haleem could be enjoyed better on its own on another occasion.

For several days, as he completed the upholstering of the sofa, Beg made plans for the fantasy banquet he'd serve. When his stitching and stretching were complete, Mrs Meer requested him: 'How about a date for the promised biryani? Could you come along and cook it here next Sunday?'

Beg agreed with alacrity. The date was fixed, and he asked for some cash in advance to buy the ingredients.

On Saturday, Mrs Meer tried to contact Beg but received no response from his mobile. She thought he had probably gone shopping. But Sunday came with still no news from Beg. Mrs Meer grew anxious. The arrangement was for Beg to come and start preparing the feast in the morning. Had he misunderstood? Perhaps he intended to cook the rice at his home and bring it over?

The guests were expected at six. No sign of Beg with his biryani. It's already four o'clock, too late to make it here, Mrs Meer said to herself. What next? I'll ring Memon Biryaniwala's restaurant and order a pot of that famous biryani of his that they've all been raving about to keep on standby.

As the guests were turning out on that freezing evening in the hope of a steaming fragrant dish of rice and lamb, serving something lesser would be an anticlimax.

It was nearly five when Beg finally rang. 'Ma'am, I'm in Birmingham refurbishing a huge mansion. New curtains, new cushions, new covers for a great number of armchairs and sofas, I'll be here for at least another week. Whatever made you think I'd be cooking for you today? Had we fixed a day, ma'am?'

'But Mr Beg, you took an advance for the shopping–'

'What advance, ma'am? Honest to God, I gratefully accepted what you gave me for my labour and I thought that you'd given me a bonus because you were pleased with my work. No date was fixed for the biryani, ma'am!'

The bell rang. Mrs Meer wearily put down the receiver and went to the door.

~

About seven years later, Mrs Meer received a call from a woman called Safia who said she was a skilled chef and could cook all the classic dishes, including biryani. A mutual acquaintance had suggested she get in touch to offer her services to Mrs Meer.

'Could you bring me a sample of your biryani to taste? What do you charge for one portion? If it's the way we like it, we'll order more.'

Safia arrived on a blustery Saturday in February. Torrents of rain had fallen in the morning; by noon the pavements were thick with snow. The phone rang and rang again. The girl seemed to have lost her way. Mrs Meer's grandson, Ali, who was visiting for the weekend and had been texting friends on his mobile, got to his feet with a groan, slipped on his shoes, threw on his overcoat and set off to look for her. He couldn't see much through the swirling sleet, but a female form emerged unexpectedly in the middle of the road in front of the building. Bundled up in a great coat, plus balaclava and boots, she was waving her arms about frantically. Ali gestured towards the entrance and she crossed over to greet him.

Small, plump and rosy-cheeked, Safia was about forty and looked like a Kashmiri. The rice she brought was fragrant, sprinkled with almonds and perhaps pistachios, and surrounded by tiny meatballs. It tasted fine, but it wasn't, in Mrs Meer's book, an authentic biryani: she'd call it a pulau. Safia was clearly a good cook though, and versatile. Mrs Meer decided to have her over to cook a meal once or twice a week.

Mrs Meer learnt that Safia was a widow. Her husband had been shot at by some mad sniper while he was strolling on a Karachi street, and had died as he waited for the ambulance a witness from a nearby stall had summoned. Their child was now with Safia's mother while she had come to London to work within a family. She wasn't only a good cook; she was also skilled at ironing, sewing and dressmaking. One day she looked at Beg's cushions and said: 'Ma'am, these covers are really old now. If you like I can make new ones for you.'

Within a week or two she produced the new covers. She said that she had made wedding dresses for various friends and neighbours in Karachi, and, though her husband didn't approve, she'd enjoyed a small income from her work. She needed additional jobs in London as the money she made working for an expat businessman's family twice a week wasn't enough to manage on in this city.

'Why don't you keep me here with you?' she'd say to Mrs Meer. 'I can take care of everything around the house. I can occasionally do other work here and there to supplement what you pay me. If you have no objection, that is.'

Mrs Meer was in a dilemma. The girl's really useful to have around, she thought. She charges a lot, but she's most capable and her confidence and ability are remarkable. But I'm not used nowadays to having someone hovering around me all day. Besides, I'll have to teach her how I like things done, and my days are fully occupied already.

So, for the time being, the question of Safia coming to live with Mrs Meer was put to one side.

~

Mrs Meer's friend Parveen was constantly in need of help around the house. Every time she heard that Mrs Meer had acquired new domestic help, she'd say: 'Do send her along to me, dear.' And that was how Safia started going to her on Tuesday mornings. Parveen was well satisfied with her work.

At about this time, Mrs Meer took it into her head that insects were crawling beneath the carpet in her bedroom. When she mentioned it to Safia, she said right away: 'Don't you worry, ma'am, I'll call someone in to take care of that.' And picking up her mobile, she began a rapid conversation in a flurry of Punjabi.

A couple of days later, Parveen rang to say: 'The silly woman hasn't shown up and I've invited two friends to lunch. Can you give me the number of a decent takeaway nearby? I can't possibly stand and cook with my arthritic knees.'

A few days went by and then Mrs Meer heard from Safia. She apologised profusely. A business magnate was over from Bombay: she had a full-time, 'live-in' job with him and needed to stay there for a few months.

'I'm so ashamed, I should have let you know. But if you should need me especially, ma'am, just call and I'll be there.'

~

Spring came and then summer, though that summer the rain hardly stopped for a day. Safia would phone now and again. Sometimes she had a job and sometimes she didn't. She had problems with her visa, but then managed to obtain a work permit. On occasions she would drop in with a delicacy Mrs Meer had ordered or she would come to do some small job around the house.

One day Mrs Meer reminded her about the need to get rid of the insects under the carpet.

'I'll get hold of the exterminators right away,' Safia said, and again there came a rapid flurry of Punjabi on her mobile.

~

A few weeks later, the exterminator called, ringing the doorbell loudly on a Sunday morning. Mohammad Ameen was an Afghan lad from Cricklewood, sturdy and green-eyed. Behind closed doors, he gave the carpet a thorough going over, but as he left, he announced that he hadn't found a single insect that needed exterminating. 'But sister, your carpet's worn out. Just say the word and we'll fit a new one.'

Mrs Meer chuckled. 'So you sell carpets too?'

'Me an' my friends do a whole lot of things. But fitting a carpet for you, I'd do it all by myself. Beg sent me over as he couldn't find anyone else to kill them insects.'

Mrs Meer made up her mind to have two rooms re-carpeted. She chose a sandalwood shade which reminded her of the shimmering golden sands of Clifton's beaches.

Ameen arrived the following Thursday and worked diligently for a few hours laying the carpet in the first room. The next day, after only a short while, he stopped work, exhausted. 'Sister, it's my first day of fasting. Aren't you fasting too? I won't be able to do all the fetching and carrying by meself. If you'll allow me to, I'll ask my mate to come and help me. But it'll cost you another thirty pound.'

There didn't seem to be much of an alternative, with the work half done and her precious objects and other bric-a-brac scattered all over the place.

'Go ahead,' Mrs Meer said.

Not long after that the doorbell rang and Ali opened the door to a woman with bobbed reddish hair, dressed in clothes that looked as if they came from a Littlewood's catalogue. He felt he'd seen her before.

'You don't recognise me, sir. Safia!'

Ali thought how much she'd changed in just a few months.

She worked purposefully with Ameen, and by evening, the second carpet was down.

~

On Saturday evening, Ali had just showered and changed to go out. At five o'clock, a colleague at his university was reading a paper on art and exile and several academics from South Asia and the diaspora were there for the conference. Safia was doing something for Mrs Meer in the kitchen when the doorbell rang. Ali hurried to the door to find Beg of the fantasy banquets standing there, lean and lanky, protruding teeth intact, his grizzled hair now quite white, though his moustache was still black. He held out his hand in greeting, but seemed not to recognise Ali. Had Ali changed that much in seven years, or was this Beg's pretence?

'I'm Beg, boss of the carpet company, come to collect my cheque,' he said.

Mrs Meer had already written out the cheque, so Ali gave it to Beg, who took it. Then he asked, 'Is Miss Safia still here?'

'Yes, come this way,' Ali said, showing him to the kitchen. Mrs Meer looked at Beg coldly, and he didn't show any sign of recognising her.

Outside, the summer rain was pouring down. Ali picked up his umbrella and left the house.

~

'She's one tough lady, our Safia,' Mrs Meer said as Ali entered, looking up from the Pakistani news she was watching on television. 'You know she cleared up all the mess after the furniture men had gone.'

Ali had come back very wet and rather disgruntled from the conference, where much time had been spent talking about a series of photographs called

'Sunrise, Sunset', taken by a Pakistani woman in the US and in Karachi. They were inspired by an Urdu children's poem that said that the cradle of the sun was in the east and its graveyard in the west; the juxtaposed images told a different story. Ali, who had lived all over the world since the age of eight and styled himself a rootless cosmopolitan, was disturbed by the photographer's advocacy of rootedness, but hadn't been given a chance to say so because there had been too little time for questions after the discussion.

'More killings in Karachi. Even in Ramadan.' Mrs Meer had switched the television off and was snipping the peel of an orange with a silver knife into fine juliennes.

'Granma, did you meet the man who was running the company?'

'The one who came for the money was the old joker Beg–'

'Uhm. However did he get hold of Safia?'

'Maybe he passed on my number to Safia to make up for the let-down over the biryani. By the way, I asked her where she lived. Kilburn, she said. "I live in Mr Beg's house now."'

'But Beg is–'

'Yes, he has a wife and three or four children.

He's just back from spending time with them in Karachi.'

'So you think he's made Safia his second wife?'

'I never asked.'

Mrs Meer was separating the orange she'd peeled into smooth segments.

'Do you think they have some sort of understanding?' Ali asked, then guffawed. 'Sounds like something from one of your Karachi soaps.'

'Can you imagine me asking her that sort of question? I'm not one of God's little soldiers. She didn't ask for my advice and I didn't offer it.'

Mrs Meer had arranged the bright orange segments on a silver platter. 'Have some,' she said, pushing the plate towards Ali.

Translated from the original Urdu 'Hauslamand' by Sabeeha Ahmed Husain, with the collaboration of Carole Smith and the author.

Knotted Tongue 1

1

One day in the first months of the twenty-first century I received a letter. It read: *I'm a poet. I'd like you to participate in my book launch and also say something about my poetry.* The writer enclosed some poems whose words were like drops of rain and arrowheads of fire. The letter came from my old country.

2

I met her: she was twenty-four and her name was Zohra. Small, with long, curly brown ringlets, and very bright. During the four or five hours we sat talking, it seemed as if we'd known each other before. It seemed as if there had been many such meetings.

3

I lived in the city and she by the sea some distance away. We'd meet sometimes but often only speak on the phone.

4

A year went by. Then the war came and engulfed us in its tribulations. Zohra said: I'm going home. I want to go home to do something. Here one's tongue is useless. The bastards seal our lips and leave our arms paralysed. I can't speak any more, neither verse nor protest. Here I'm a vagabond, I carry my home on my back. Once home, my deprivation will become my language of freedom. I want to write poems in my mother tongue.

5

Zohra went back. Poems would arrive from our country, and letters too.

6

Another year went by and Zohra came back to this city. She said: There each sound gets stuck in my throat. One can't even sing, let alone shout. Better for me to stay away for a while from our homeland. If I could just find a job ...

7

She brought gifts, among which were recordings of ragas played on the sarod and the veena. After she left me, I listened to them all night long.

8

Once we set off together on a bus journey. In a distant town, following the literary event, someone spoke in favour of the war and her temper flared. On the bus journey back, she slept with her head pressed against the window.

When she woke, it was dark outside, no moon, no stars. She said: It's happening again here. Knots in my tongue. But at home each sound gets stuck in my throat. I can no longer speak, let alone write poetry. If I could just find a job ... I'll be twenty-eight soon. I'm losing my mother tongue. I'm a vagabond, I carry my home on my back. Now I shall turn this foreign tongue into a whip and lash them with their words.

9

In a glass hall on the banks of the river, one afternoon. White swans skimmed the surface of the water. She'd gathered her thoughts into poems and read aloud two of them. Then said to me, You read the rest. People heard her poems and were moved. That afternoon I told her about a job. I said: I'll take you. Let's travel together.

10

The day before our trip, a friend called. Zohra had been injured in a traffic accident. A car had collided with a motorcycle. The driver left her unconscious on the road and ran away. Her friend said: She's in hospital. She's just come to. She's thinking of you. She says you must come to see her when she's a little better.

11

Two days later, he called again. Zohra had left us. They were sending her body home.

12

A friend of hers came to see me some days later. She said: When it was your birthday a few months ago I went with Zohra to look for a gift. We tramped around many shops. Zohra said, What can I buy him? He has everything. Books. Paintings. Then she heard the sound of the sarod in the market. Listen, she said. Yes, he'll like that! And she went off in search of those notes.

Translated from the original Urdu 'Do Kahaniyan: Zohra' by the author and Carole Smith.

Knotted Tongue 2

1

That day Shams and I sat on the train and talked endlessly. The landscape outside was shrouded in floodwater. It was July, but there had been floods.

2

We travelled for seven hours and reached the town on the edge of the river at five. The sun was still high and the roofs of the tall fort-like buildings glowed in its rays. At once we set off to wander the lanes of the unknown town. The river had broken its banks and several streets were under water.

3

After the literary festival that evening and the next morning, we made the same long journey back. Shams said, I brought along a book but I'm not in the mood to read, let's talk. We talked and talked, and outside the rainwater still submerged the fields. Once it seemed as if the branches of a drowning tree were making gestures to the sky but we talked on and on.

4

I'd known Shams for thirty-five years. When we first met I was seventeen and she was about thirty-five. We both liked singing and poetry. Then there was a revolution in her country, and traitors took over mine. At thirty, I gave up singing, and some years later, she did too. She'd had some successes, but I was too shy and too busy to look for fame. We also began to write at about the same time. I wrote stories and she accounts of her life. People remarked to us both: You colour your writings with exile.

5

Some time ago we'd had a misunderstanding. It was on her side. But during that long journey, she didn't refer to it, and neither did I. Perhaps silent anger can be washed away by rainwater. I remember Shams saying, What a worry it is, this having to make a living wage, it kills you. I'm far away from my country, far away from my faith, I don't want to die alone in this desolate city.

6

When we said goodbye I saw regret in her eyes.

7

I met Shams once again after that journey. She took me to dinner. She thanked me for many things, but I couldn't understand what her gratitude was for.

8

One day in winter, a weeping friend told me, Shams is ill. A flood of worries has swallowed her up. It had snowed that day.

9

Shams and I spoke only once more. On the phone. Again, her grateful words; then she said, When I'm a little better you must come and see me.

10

But just before spring arrived, she died.

11

She left no will. But a friend said she had given verbal instructions that she wanted fire, not earth, as her final element.

Translated from the original Urdu 'Do Kahaniyan: Shams Khanum' by the author and Carole Smith.

37 Bridges

1

'Take me to the river,' I said to Nermin when we met at the Gare de Nord.

2

I've always loved rivers, and cities through which they pass. Cities are often too remote from rivers, or the river runs dry and leaves only a trickle of water that looks like a stream. I've seen a dried-up river bed in Delhi, where the washermen wash clothes in the yellow trickle, and people plant watermelons which they sell on the streets in summer. In Lahore too, the river looks feeble and muddy. The grandest view is in

Istanbul, but the lashing blue Bosphorus isn't a river, it's a strait, which divides the city in two like a river would.

I first met Nermin in Istanbul four years ago. She seemed quite settled there. She didn't agree with much of what her friends were saying about Erdogan.

'Let's wait and watch,' she'd say. 'I'm happy here because this city doesn't lay any claim on me. Perhaps your relationship with London's like that? I was neither born nor brought up here. When fighting broke out in Cyprus I was only nine or ten. Turkish was my language and I spoke it well, but even today I use some words like a Cypriot would. Then I got married at twenty and moved to the States where I lived for many years with my husband.'

3

Now, after four years, we were meeting in Paris. Since the last time I'd seen her, Nermin had been wandering around the world. Europe, America, Australia. A month ago she'd written to me: *I've said farewell to Istanbul. I've given back the place to the landlady and come to Paris.*

She'd moved into her own little flat. On the phone, she'd said: 'I'm off to America in a few weeks and I'm going to be there for two months. Why don't you come and see me?'

'This is my busy time. I'm marking student papers.'

'It's a bank holiday next Monday. Just come over for a day. You can take the train back in the evening.'

4

I'd boarded the train in the morning, early. Two hours on the Eurostar and I was in Paris. The station was crowded and I didn't see her. In a panic, I called her on her cellphone and there was no reply. I hadn't been in Paris for thirty-three years and I was a complete stranger here. I wondered what I'd do if I didn't find her.

Then someone called out my name. I turned to see Nermin running towards me in a red dress.

5

'There are thirty-seven bridges in Paris,' she said as she led me to the river. 'Let's have lunch first, then I'll take you to the river.'

We stopped under the awning of Shakespeare's bookshop opposite the Gothic white fantasy of Notre Dame. We sat down on the open terrace of a restaurant nearby and talked. I felt as if I'd done nothing more in all these years than travel, teach and write a few stories. A lot had happened to Nermin, though. Just a few days after the last time I'd seen her in Istanbul, she'd left her husband and moved into her own flat. Her son was eighteen or nineteen and engrossed in his studies. She couldn't take him with her, but she didn't want to be too far from him. So she'd found a little room nearby. Now her son was twenty-three. He'd moved to Paris after completing his studies; Nermin had been travelling back and forth. After the events at Gezi Park, she'd become disheartened with the divisions around her. Social divisions. Political factions. Ideological and religious factions. She'd started to feel she wasn't any part of it.

'It isn't entirely dark,' she'd said, 'but the storm clouds are gathering.'

6

Meanwhile she'd written some of her most beautiful stories, almost prose poems. Stories about brothers and sisters parting, about friendships breaking up over a child's broken toy, about passionate attachments born in the tumult of a political demonstration.

Brief, slight images, like the breath of a bird dying on the sleeve of the wind, like the castanets of a dancing gypsy, like a drop of blood from the paw of a wounded rabbit in the grass, like the last smouldering embers of the evening.

7

We crossed the church gardens and came to a bridge.

'Stop here, I'll take a photograph.' she said.

The filigreed walls of the bridge were laden with bunches of artificial flowers in bright colours: red, yellow, blue, purple.

There were cloud reflections in the river's grey waters.

As I walked towards the wall I noticed that what I'd thought were flowers weren't flowers at all, they were locks: bunches of locks, big locks, small locks, heavy locks, little locks. Locks of all sizes, locks of all colours.

Nermin was laughing.

'Don't you know the story of this bridge?'

'No. Tell me.'

'You really don't know? This is the Archbishop's Bridge, but now it's known as the Bridge of Lovers! Young lovers come here in the middle of the night, swear fidelity to each other, fasten a lock on the wall, lock it up and throw away the key into the Seine. No one can trace the origins of this custom. It's predicted that weight of the locks will bring the walls down one day. Two American women recently filed a complaint about it. They even tried to break the locks with a hammer but the locks won't break. And all the keys are in the depths of the river.'

'Isn't there a young bride in one of your stories who comes to Paris with her husband? She got married to him against her parents' wishes. Wandering around the streets of Paris they get into an argument. They reach a bridge and the husband threatens to jump into the river.'

'Yes, this is the bridge. I came here on my honeymoon. It was a snowy winter night, but I didn't see any locks here then. And we didn't make any vows here or swear to stay together forever. Well, all that ... come on, let's move on, it's getting late.'

8

A metro journey in the afternoon's rush hour. Don't people have showers here? There are quite a few beggars in this opulent city, hanging around the station and the street corners. But then it occurs to me that we are all strangers in these cities of ours, and strangers we'll remain.

We got off the metro. The afternoon was mild. We sat over an espresso in the shade of a tree. Two veiled African women passed by.

'No one takes me for a Muslim here,' Nermin said, sipping her coffee.

'So, should all Muslims be wandering around wrapped in a sheet?' I asked.

'But you're not an Arab, they say. Not all the world's Muslims are Arab, I retort. But you're so fair, and your hair is brown ... What can I say to that, except for wishing I was brown too.'

'I'd gone to dinner at a friend's', I said. 'An academic historian was trying to pick an argument about veiled women with the hostess, who writes about Mughal art. To begin with, the lady tried to keep the conversation light, citing relative cultural values etc. Then I realised that the esteemed professor was trying to pull me into the argument. He addressed me directly and said: In early days, migrants used to bring the seeds of their own progress with them which they planted in the new soil. Look at the Jews in America. Look at the children of immigrants. The sons of the illiterate became scientists and political theorist. But your Muslims have reversed the process!

They come to the West with their antediluvian customs and want everyone to kowtow to them. They are squandering all our capital ...'

I had noticed that he'd been drinking quite a bit; I gave him a sharp response with references to the Second World War and then changed the subject. And I remembered how the election of Modi had driven a young friend of mine to consider abandoning his research in India to come back to London. Someone had told him that if he didn't like India, he should go and blow himself up across the border. *Living there's becoming unbearable*, he'd written. *Even one's friends are becoming strangers.*

I was waiting for Nermin's response to my unspoken question: What brought you away from Istanbul, where you could call so many your own? Perhaps your memories are redolent of the island where you witnessed so many kinds of prejudice. Religion. Nation. Ethnic identity. And you couldn't escape these memories. But my wandering thoughts had taken me away from where we were. The evening was on the wane and soon I'd have to catch my train.

'Whenever I felt a bit anxious in Istanbul, I'd look out from my window at the Bosphorus,' Nermin's voice interrupted my reverie. 'But after the riots, I didn't feel too safe walking around alone in the evenings. Here, on the other hand, I spend evenings strolling on the riverbanks. From one bridge to another. The sun doesn't set till ten in June. I think as I wander. Faint outlines and broken phrases of new stories arise in my mind. But when I get home and sit down at my desk, so many of those sounds and images have just slipped away. All the stories are lying around unfinished. But, listen, aren't you seeing anyone these days?'

I was about to tell her. Instead I smiled and said: 'Where do I have the time for emotional entanglements?'

9

So many stories remained untold during this short interlude, stories I'd wanted to tell her. I just said, You'll be off to America now, then what's next?

'This state of homelessness here – you could say that's where I feel most at home.'

She laughed. It was nearly time for me to leave for the station.

'Let's go home,' she said. 'It's not far. We can have some bread and cheese for supper before you take your train.'

10

There were only eleven minutes left for the train to depart when I took my seat. Two hours to London, and then another three quarters of an hour to reach home, it'll be midnight by the time I get in. I took out my notes for tomorrow's lecture from my bag. I had another long train journey tomorrow and then my classes.

Along with the pleasure of seeing Nermin I also felt a light sadness. Home, estrangement, faith, love – how we wander around in these tight concentric circles. Outside the sky was a fiery gold at 10 p.m. When will it be night? After seeing me off, Nermin must be strolling down the bridges of Paris: from one bridge to another in her red dress. Perhaps she'll walk from the lovers' bridge to the bridge of partings and then she'll reach her door. I closed my stinging eyes. 'Guess what I did when I got to Paris?' The gentle echo of Nermin's words was in my ears. 'I stood on the bridge and emptied my pockets of all the keys that I'd been carrying around in my pockets and purses for years and years. Keys to which I'd long ago lost the locks and I didn't even know where they came from. House keys. Keys to things left behind when I'd changed houses. Keys to wardrobes, chests of drawers, trunks. Keys of cars I'd driven long ago.'

But which of the thirty-seven bridges of Paris was it that she stood on when she threw away the keys? Not the bridge of lovers? I too have a key in my pocket and I have no idea to which door it belongs. Every time I look for something in that pocket my hand finds the same key. I'd like to throw it away in the river, I wanted to say, but Nermin wasn't with me. And perhaps in my drowsiness I'd heard her say something she never said.

The train plunged into darkness as it entered the tunnel beneath the sea. On the other side was the border with England. I shut my eyes again.

Translated from the Urdu 'Saintis Pul' by Sabeeha Ahmed Husain and the author.

Acknowledgements

Earlier versions of some of these stories first appeared in *Critical Muslim, Molossus, Moth, The New Statesman, Bengal Lights*, and the anthologies *Still* and *xo Orpheus*. I thank all the editors, particularly Samira Shackle, Robin Yassin-Kassab, Ziauddin Sardar, Roelof Bakker, Chandrahas Chaudhury, K. Anis Ahmed, Khademul Islam, Ahsan Akbar, Sascha Akhtar, Sudeep Sen, Rebecca O'Connor and Kate Bernheimer, for eliciting these stories.

I originally wrote four of these stories in Urdu, albeit in different versions; they were published in *Dunyazad 36*. My thanks to Asif Farrukhi for his enthusiasm and encouragement, and to Carole Smith, my colleague, for her beautiful English versions of some of these stories, which she encouraged me to translate.

I am particularly grateful to my mother, Sabeeha Ahmed Husain, for teaching me the Urdu language from which I so often draw inspiration, and for her contribution to, and wonderful impromptu translation of 'The Entrepreneurs'.

And special thanks to Alev for her verbal and visual collaboration on the Andalusian story.

I'd also like to thank my first readers for their unflagging interest, support and affection: Mimi Khalvati, Hanan al-Shaykh and Ruth Padel. Thanks too to the members of Kindlings, and all the other friends along the way who asked for stories, and special thanks to Iman Humaydan for Paris and the story of the bridge.